CLUB TIMES

For Members' Eyes Only

Dr. Sweetheart and flying snail shells...

Nothing makes me giddier than a man who appreciates a good joke. And Dr. Jared Cross certainly made my heart go pitter-pat when he listened to me tell the one about the rabbi, the priest, the go-go dancer and the nun. I got a little lost in my story while staring at his wild green eyes and gleaming smile. I kept thinking that Dr. Cross needed a good woman—someone to ruffle up his hair and give him some roses to smell. And then I forgot the punch line.

Harvey Small wanted me to announce that he's giving etiquette classes on Tuesday nights. I won't mention that Harv slammed the door in my face last week. Then again, maybe he didn't enjoy my exposé on country club managers and hair loss. Make sure to bring an extra plastic fork and your escargot equipment for each class. And please leave the

kids at home. The class was reprimanded for beaning Ford Carson with empty snail shells.

Time to run! Gotta go catch famous heiress Melanie Tourbier, who's just arrived and made a beeline for Dr. Cross's office. Wonder what that could be about!

Make the Lone Star Country Club your private getaway. The Jacuzzi's waiting....

About the Author

ELIZABETH HARBISON

began her love affair with Texas when her sister moved
there in the early 1980s. It's a place she's revisited, both
in fiction and in life, several times, and she always loves
to return. Writing *Mission Creek Mother-To-Be* was
a particular pleasure, since it incorporated some of
Elizabeth's favorite themes: a runaway heiress, babies,
a tortured hero who needs love and a happy ending.

ELIZABETH HARBISON

MISSION CREEK
MOTHER-TO-BE

Published by Silhouette Books
America's Publisher of Contemporary Romance

Special thanks and acknowledgment are given to Elizabeth Harbison for her contribution to the LONE STAR COUNTRY CLUB series.

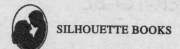

SILHOUETTE BOOKS

ISBN 0-373-61365-2

MISSION CREEK MOTHER-TO-BE

Visit Silhouette at www.eHarlequin.com

Printed in U.S.A.

Welcome to the

LONE STAR
LC
COUNTRY CLUB
EST. 1923

Where Texas society reigns supreme—
and appearances are everything.

She didn't think she wanted a baby
the old-fashioned way until she met a doctor
who had just the right bedside manner!

Dr. Jared Cross: As a fertility counselor and child psychiatrist, the good doctor makes dreams come true for so many families. But it's his work with one woman in particular that has him thinking of a future—and a family—of his very own.

Melanie Tourbier: She's been surrounded by gold-digging men her entire life. Now, with her desire for a baby increasing by the minute, Melanie knows a fertility clinic is her best option. Except there's a very special doctor in attendance who's making her rethink her child's paternity....

Fireworks in Mission Creek: An explosion outside the nursery of Mission Creek Memorial Hospital and the escape of a vengeful criminal lead to a dangerous hostage situation. Whose lives will be spared...and who will suffer to protect others?

THE FAMILIES

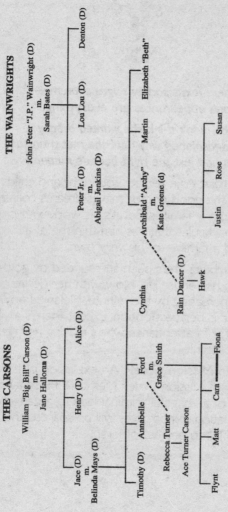

THE CARSONS

William "Big Bill" Carson (D)
m.
Jane Halloran (D)

- Jace (D) — m. Belinda Mays (D)
- Henry (D)
- Alice (D)

- Timothy (D)
- Annabelle
- Ford — m. Grace Smith
- Cynthia

Rebecca Turner
Ace Turner Carson

Rain Dancer (D)
- Hawk

- Flynt
- Matt
- Cara
- Fiona

THE WAINWRIGHTS

John Peter "J.P." Wainwright (D)
m.
Sarah Bates (D)

- Peter Jr. (D) — m. Abigail Jenkins (D)
- Lou Lou (D)
- Denton (D)

- Archibald "Archy" — m. Kate Greene (d)
- Martin
- Elizabeth "Beth"

- Justin
- Rose
- Susan

D Deceased
d Divorced
m. Married
--- Affair
━━ Twins

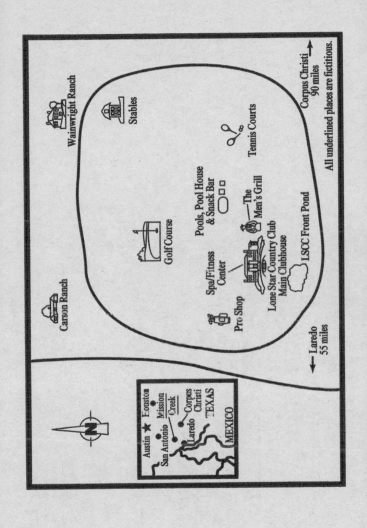

To Greg Cunliffe
The Godfather

One

" *...Branson Hines has escaped from authorities while being transferred from Mission Creek to a high-security prison in Lubbock. The thirty-two-year-old Hines is described as five feet ten inches tall, with dark eyes, dirty-blond hair and an unkempt goatee. Police spokesman Darryl Reilly warns that Hines is volatile and may be armed. Anyone who knows anything about his whereabouts is requested to call the Mission Creek Police hot line at—* "

Melanie Tourbier reached out and clicked off the radio of her rented convertible. Then she shuddered and tried to take a deep cleansing breath as her yoga teacher in London had instructed. If things were going to work out the way she wanted them to here in Mission Creek, she needed to relax, to think positive thoughts. She did not need to panic about a dangerous escaped criminal who happened to be on the loose in the very small town she was staying in for the next few weeks. She'd be cautious, of course. But then, she was always cautious about strangers.

A lifetime's worth of paparazzi and gold diggers had taught her that.

Her cell phone rang on the seat next to her and she

punched the "on" button, glad for the distraction. She slipped the hands-free earpiece into her ear. She was nothing if not safety conscious. "Hello?"

"Where *are* you?"

Melanie smiled at the voice of her friend Jeff. She could picture him in her mind, his wavy brown hair mussed, his thin body draped casually across the Chippendale chair he'd inherited from his wealthy grandfather. "You know where I am," she said. "I'm in Texas."

"Melanie Tourbier, you are out of your mind! Come back before it's too late."

"It's already too late. I've made up my mind and I'm going through with this." She readjusted her grip on the steering wheel, symbolically reconfirming her resolution. "Face it, pal, you're going to be an honorary uncle."

"Much as I'd love that, I think you're going about this the wrong way."

"No, I'm not," she said lightly. She was certain of that.

"But you're only thirty!" Jeff argued. "You've got plenty of time to meet a man the traditional way, not in a test tube."

"Oh, Jeff, don't be silly, they don't keep men in test tubes here," she teased.

"They keep the *essence* of them there, and don't change the subject. You've got plenty of time to go about this in the usual way and you know it."

"I already tried that."

"One bad husband doesn't mean that there's no one good out there."

Melanie laughed. "Maybe not, but it certainly opened my eyes to some of the bad that's out there."

"Your relationship with Michael wasn't all bad."

"Bad enough." Michael Mason had entered her life as a financial advisor and had left it as a financial liability. The divorce had cost her millions, but it was worth it to get rid of a man who had become more domineering and intimidating with every passing month. The only good thing, if you could call it good, that had come from the relationship was she'd learned early on about medical problems that would make it very difficult for her to conceive a child. One doctor had given her a one-in-a-hundred chance, though to her it felt like one in a million.

Which was a main reason she'd decided upon her current course of action.

"Why not just wait a couple of years?" Jeff implored. "Mr. Right might be just around the corner."

"Even if he was, and I know he's not, a couple of years won't do it." She tapped her foot on the brakes and glanced right and left as she rolled over some railroad tracks. "Think about it. Say, hypothetically, I meet a guy today. We'd have to date for at least a year before I could trust him enough to even *consider* sleeping with him—"

"A year?"

"At least. Remember what happened with Roberto?"

"Ah, yes, the pool boy."

"He wasn't a pool boy and you know it. He was the landscape artist. And a con artist," she added miserably. Roberto Loren had been a huge mistake. A flirtation gone out of control. Melanie had met him when he'd come to redesign the grounds of her estate in Maui. They'd spent the summer flirting and dating, and eventually took a trip to his home in Majorca together, where she found out, the hard way, two crucial facts: first, that Roberto was not divorced as he'd said but still quite married with three young children; and second, that he'd set the whole thing up so he could have scandalous-looking pictures taken poolside, with his children present, which he could sell to the tabloids.

His trashy book on the affair was due to hit the stores this week.

"Okay, I can see why you'd want to take some time to get to know and trust a man," Jeff conceded. "Maybe do a background check. I'll give you a year for that."

"Right," she said. "So I'm thirty-one right there. Then there's the time spent trying to get pregnant. You know about my problems there. I already tried for two years with Michael, to no avail. And I was younger then. It could take three, four years now, or even more."

"Or a month."

Melanie scoffed. "Those odds are a million to one, as you well know. And with every year that passes, conception grows more difficult. The already minuscule window of opportunity gets smaller and smaller, and the risk of birth complications increases dramatically.'' She'd memorized these arguments over the past year of repeating them to herself. "Now, where was I?''

"You were almost forty, I think.''

"Right.'' There was a blue hospital sign ahead and Melanie slowed the car and stopped at a red light. "And that's just the first child. What if I want more?'' She felt the questioning gaze of the person in the car next to her and lowered her voice. "I'd have to start all over again with—''

"Stop!'' Jeff cried into the receiver, just as the stoplight turned green.

Melanie pressed the accelerator, turned the car left onto Mission Creek Drive and kept her eyes open for Mission Creek Memorial Hospital. "I've made myself clear, then?''

"Crystal.'' He sounded defeated, but she knew Jeff well enough to know he'd resurrect the subject countless times before it was truly too late. "So how is Texas?''

"Hot,'' Melanie answered, tipping her face gratefully toward the summer sun. "Wonderfully hot and sunny. I may never leave.''

"That's exactly what I was afraid of when you left London. You may have lived here for the past fifteen years or so, but you're still an American at heart.''

"And on my passport,'' Melanie added. She'd

grown up in the United States, living first in San Francisco and then in Dallas from ages five to fourteen. After her parents' death when she was just fifteen, she had lived primarily in London, first attending an exclusive girls boarding school on the orders of her parents' executor, then, after a brief stint at the Cordon Bleu in Paris, returning to the University of London where she studied art history.

She'd married Michael Turner directly after graduating. They had divorced just under three years later. In the ensuing five years, Melanie had focused her energies on the many charitable organizations her parents had established and patronized, but her life still felt empty. Despite everything she had, all she truly wanted was a family. Her optimism about that was fading fast. It didn't help that the only men she'd met since her divorce were either party boys or opportunists, after her money and fame.

So Melanie decided she was through with men, through with romance. She did, however, still want a family of her own. So she'd done some research and learned that the fertility clinic at Mission Creek Memorial Hospital was one of the best in the world, as well as one of the most discreet. She'd come in part because of the clinic's reputation and in part because, after all these years, she was finally ready to come home. Texas still felt like home.

"So what are you doing right now?" Jeff wanted to know.

"Right now I'm in the car. I'm on my way to meet

with a family planning counselor," she said. "A Dr. Cross. Doesn't he sound nice? As I understand it, I have a quick chat with him, assure him that I know what I'm doing, and then *bingo,* I'm off for the procedure. Or at least the first one." She smiled at the thought, although she was well aware she might need multiple tries. Still she felt it was best to be optimistic. "Who knows? Next time you hear from me, I might be pregnant!" She hung up the phone and returned her full attention to the road before her, literally and metaphorically.

When she arrived at the hospital, she strode straight to the elevator, pressing the button with a flourish. "One step closer," she said excitedly under her breath.

"I beg your pardon?"

Startled, she whirled to see a man standing there. He was tall and dark, with the most striking pale-green eyes she'd ever seen. "I—I was just talking to myself."

"Oh. Sorry. Didn't mean to eavesdrop."

She smiled. "I guess someone who's talking to herself has to accept eavesdroppers as part of the deal and hope none of them is a psychiatrist."

He gave her a strange smile, and she immediately thought her joke was idiotic. Now he probably thought she was, too.

"Just kidding," she added, in case there was any doubt.

"That's what I figured."

His eyes were mesmerizing, like a hypnotist's watch. She couldn't look away.

He was looking at her, too, and he frowned slightly, as if trying to place her. "I'm sorry, but do we know each other?"

"No, no. I don't think so. But you do look... familiar," she finished lamely. He didn't look familiar at all. This was not a face she would have forgotten.

The bell dinged behind her, and she heard the elevator doors shoosh open. She turned and walked into the mirrored elevator, conscious not so much of the thirty Melanies that seemed to step on with her, but the thirty tall, dark-haired, green-eyed strangers.

She reached out to press the eighth-floor button at the same time he did on the opposite side of the door. She glanced at him and said with a nervous little laugh, "Popular floor."

He smiled. "Most of the offices are there. Patient rooms are on the other floors."

"Oh." She shrugged. "I'm not familiar with the building. This is my first time here."

"Where are you headed?"

"To see Dr.—" She stopped, reflexively protecting her privacy. "A specialist." She gave a dismissive smile and watched the numbers as the elevator climbed.

The man nodded politely and didn't ask questions.

It occurred to her then that she wasn't entirely sure which suite she was headed for. Glad for the chance to do something other than say inane things to a stranger, she opened her purse and began rooting for the appointment card they'd sent to her in England.

As the elevator lurched to a stop, she dropped her wallet at the man's feet. She reached for it at the precise moment he did and they bumped heads just as the elevator doors opened.

"Sorry," Melanie said, her embarrassment increasing with every moment.

He laughed and handed her the wallet, which had ended up in his hand like the big end of a wishbone. His fingertips brushed hers. "Nice bumping into you." He gave an attractive grin.

She groaned at the pun as they both stepped off the elevator. Then she retrieved the appointment card from her wallet.

The stranger stopped, considered her for a moment, then asked, "Can I help you find an office at least?"

"That's okay." She pulled the card out and waved it triumphantly. "I've got it. But thanks."

"All right. Good luck." He nodded and waved and was off.

Melanie watched him go, vaguely hoping she might meet him again. Something about him was interesting, reassuring. She shrugged off the notion, and looked closely at Dr. Cross's business card. Suite 818. Once the card was back in her bag, she followed the signs to her destination.

Five minutes later Melanie was sitting in the waiting room of Dr. Jared Cross's office, trying to ignore the continuing radio coverage of Branson Hines's escape. The announcer repeated warnings that citizens may be in danger, then returned to the Muzak program with an old Barry Manilow song.

Melanie tried to keep her thoughts on the fashion magazine she'd brought, but for some reason the Branson Hines story made her feel as if she, personally, were in danger. She'd only had premonitions a couple of times in her life; once before her parents died, and once when she was in college and she was sure she was going to fail a course. She'd been wrong about the latter, so she was probably wrong about this, too.

"Miss Tourbier?"

Melanie jumped, even though the voice was soft. "Yes?" she asked the petite red-haired secretary who had called her name.

"The doctor will see you now." She gestured toward the door next to her desk.

Melanie gathered her things and gave a brief smile. "Thank you."

"Say, did you know there's a Tourbier champagne?" the secretary asked as Melanie walked past. "My husband and I had some just last night for our anniversary."

"Well, happy anniversary," Melanie said with a smile. Yes, she knew about Tourbier champagne. Her father had started the vineyard in Reims, France, thirty-three years ago.

"Thanks!" the woman answered with a shake of her flame-red curls. "Two years and counting."

"That's terrific."

She passed the young woman and entered Dr. Cross's office.

He was standing with his back to her, facing a wide shelf that was overflowing with books. She couldn't tell much about him from behind except that he was very tall, and his hair was as black as a raven's, or at least it seemed so in contrast to the generic white doctor coat he wore. His hair color and his physique suggested that he was much younger than she had expected.

"Dr. Cross?"

He turned quickly. "I'm sorry," he said, flashing an apologetic smile.

It was the man from the elevator.

Her heart dropped into her stomach. "It's you," she heard herself say. "I had no idea..."

He looked equally surprised to see her. "Oh, hello again."

"Hello."

"What a coincidence."

She swallowed. "Yes." Things like this happened a lot in her life. She really shouldn't continue to be so surprised by them.

He glanced at something on his desk and said, "I gather you must be Melanie Tourbier?"

"Yes, I am."

He looked at her for a moment, as cool as a cu-

cumber. "Please," he said, waving a hand at the chair in front of his desk. "Have a seat."

She did, wondering if he was right now recalling her talking to herself before.

That would not bode well for her.

But if he was thinking that, he didn't let on. He sat and took out a folder. "So you are Miss Tourbier," he said, taking a few sheets of paper out of the folder.

"Please, call me Melanie." A flirty thrill ran down her spine, and she quickly reminded herself that this was not the time or the place or the man for those kinds of thoughts.

He looked at her over the papers. "Okay, Melanie. And you can call me Jared."

"All right, Jared." Still, maybe this was going to go well, after all.

He frowned and checked his notes, shuffling through the papers. "And you're here for fertility counseling, is that correct? Artificial insemination?"

"Yes, I am."

He looked at her again, then hesitated noticeably before setting the papers down.

She thought she saw a piece of newspaper in the pile and wondered what it was.

"I haven't had a lot of time to familiarize myself with your case," he said. "I understand this has all happened rather quickly."

She smiled. "Why wait around?"

"Hmm." He didn't return her smile, but instead made a quick note on the top paper and returned his gaze to her. "Why don't you begin by telling me why you want to undergo this procedure at this time."

Melanie shifted uncomfortably in her seat. Something told her this wasn't going to go as smoothly as she'd expected. She hadn't planned on having to explain herself. "Because I want to start a family."

"Alone?"

"I'm not married, if that's what you mean." She cleared her throat gently.

"No…significant other?"

"No, this is something I'll be going about alone."

He nodded, studying her with those disconcertingly green eyes. "Why have you decided on this particular route at the age of—" he glanced at the papers "—just thirty?"

She straightened her back. All feelings of flirtiness had left her. Now she was firmly on the defense. "Forgive me, but I'm not sure that's any of your concern. My reasons are private."

"Whatever you tell me will be kept in confidence, I assure you."

"That's not the point."

He remained imperturbable. "What is the point, then?"

"The point," she said, with more patience than she felt, "is that this is a very personal decision, made for very personal reasons. I came here for a medical procedure, not to justify myself. But please rest assured that I gave it a great deal of serious thought."

"That's what I'm here to help you with," he said,

with more patience than she suspected he felt. "To make sure the decision you've reached is the right one for everyone involved."

"But I don't need help with that." Her patience slipped a notch. "As I said, I've already made the decision."

"Miss Tourbier," Dr. Cross said, then leaned back in his chair and scrutinized her like Columbus surveying the land ahead and wondering why the West Indies didn't look right, "the Mission Creek Clinic requires that every patient have counseling before taking this very serious step. It's vitally important that we are all in agreement that this is an appropriate action for you to take."

He made it sound like a legal issue instead of one of the heart. "I assure you, I'm capable of making decisions for myself. And the reason I'm here is for a medical procedure, not a psychological one."

He leaned forward, piercing her with a gaze that suddenly wasn't attractive so much as intimidating. "With all due respect, Miss Tourbier, it is not you that I am primarily concerned with. I agree that you are old enough to take care of yourself. My concern is for the child you wish to have."

Melanie felt as if she'd been slapped. He may not have put it as kindly as he could have, but he was right. Of course this was about the welfare of the child. She'd come across as a selfish, spoiled brat, talking about herself and what she wanted. In all her years of being alone, she'd had only herself to worry about, but she knew once the child was real, it would be second nature for her to put him or her above all else.

"Dr. Cross," she said, wishing she had an olive branch to extend, "I'm afraid we've gotten off to a bad start here. Not only do I agree that the needs of the child come first, but I appreciate the fact that you feel so strongly about it. I feel the same way."

"Do you?"

"Yes, absolutely. This is not a decision I made lightly. I had to ask myself a lot of questions first, about whether I was ready to take on such a large responsibility. Which I am," she hastened to add. "And about whether it was fair to bring a baby into the world without a father."

He nodded, looking more interested than he had when she'd begun. "And what was your answer to that last question?"

She swallowed. Maybe she shouldn't have brought that up. If she hadn't, maybe he wouldn't have thought to do it, either. "Well, I guess my answer is that I think any child is lucky to have one adoring parent. Some don't have any." She felt a pang of loss before she even realized she was thinking of her own parents. It was like that sometimes, her reaction to the loss so automatic that it came before any thought.

"I agree." Dr. Cross's voice was quiet. "There is nothing worse for a child than to feel unwanted."

"Believe me, this baby will feel wanted and loved. He or she will have more loving attention than most kids. I have…means," she understated. "I'm fortunate in that I won't have to go to work and put my baby into someone else's care. I'll be there for him twenty-four hours a day." She hesitated. "I believe that's a tremendous advantage for him. Or her."

A moment passed before he spoke again. "Miss Tourbier, I'm not going to play games. I am aware of your financial advantages. One of my concerns, though, is that a baby might seem to you to be a fun thing to have around, something to cuddle and play with, when in fact a baby is only a baby for a short period of time. Having a child is a lifetime commitment."

"Dr. Cross, I'm not a teenager looking for something to comfort adolescent angst. I'm a grown woman who has contemplated this and made a careful decision."

"And I want to help make sure it's the right one."

"But I don't need help with that, since, as I've said, I've already made the decision." Half an hour ago she'd hoped she'd meet this man again. Now he was turning into the biggest obstacle to her plan. Be careful what you wish for, she thought.

"Please understand, here at the clinic we like this to be a cooperative process."

"Well, I'm trying to cooperate, but I feel like I'm up against some stiff opposition and I'm not sure why."

He kept his gaze steady on her. "What you perceive as opposition is simply caution."

"And what is it about me that makes you feel so cautious?"

"You are a young woman seeking to raise a child alone."

"Why is that so shocking?"

"Not shocking," he said in a measured tone. "But only about five percent of our cases are single mothers."

"And do all of them undergo such scrutiny?"

"Every one of them."

"It's a wonder you've stayed in business, then."

"It's one of the reasons *why* business is thriving here. Our standards are high for both our patients and—" he paused "—our donors."

Melanie's face felt very hot. She knew they were picky about their donors, of course. That was why she'd chosen this particular clinic. She didn't want sperm from some guy who was trying to make a quick five bucks to support his drinking or drug habit. She wanted the father of her baby to be someone who was carefully screened.

"All right, let's cut to the chase," Melanie said. "What are you worried about in my case?"

"It's not easy to be a single mother. I'm afraid the reality of parenting might be a bit different from what you expect. Although you're not the first single woman to want to conceive, you are young and clearly used to a lifestyle that allows you unusual freedom."

"What's your point?"

"What happens if it all turns out to be much harder, and maybe a lot less enjoyable, than you expect?"

"I'm sure at times it will be," she said steadily. "And at those times I will love my child just the same." She chose her words carefully. "Dr. Cross, life is often not what we expect. I have learned that several times over. But I would never, ever take on a responsibility like this if I wasn't ready to give it one hundred percent."

"I'm glad to hear that." His voice softened and he scribbled something in her folder. "Honestly, I am. However, I'm sure you understand that we need to explore this further. It's our standard operating procedure."

She glanced at the desk. Did he have some sort of checklist he had to go through? "Okay," she said, resigned. "Explore away. We'll do it your way. I want you to feel as comfortable with this as I do."

He gave her the look a teacher might give a mischievous child. "Now you're suddenly feeling cooperative?"

"I'm suddenly feeling that I have no choice."

He shrugged and gave her a quick smile. "That will do, I guess. So tell me, do you have any experience with children?"

She felt her cheeks grow warm. "Not exactly."

"Hmm." He leaned his elbows on the desk and steepled his fingers before his face. "What do you mean 'not exactly'?"

"Does a person have to have experience with children in order to have one?" she countered.

"Not necessarily—"

"Good. Because I'm perfectly willing to learn on the job."

He kept his eyes on her for a moment, then made another note. She tried to see what he was writing but couldn't.

"Am I getting points against me for that?" she asked. "What are you writing?"

He looked at her with exaggerated patience. "I'm just making a few notes to myself."

"Care to share them?"

He looked at his pad, then set it down. "Okay. You want me to be blunt, I'll be blunt. I don't think you know what you're getting into. It may not be what you expect, and if it's not what you expect, your disappointment may become evident to the child. The best way to fix a mistake is not to make it in the first place."

"Dr. Cross." Melanie used her most authoritative voice. "While I do appreciate your candor, it doesn't sound to me as if you're trying to help me make this decision at all. It sounds as if you're trying to talk me out of it."

He raised an eyebrow. "Does it?"

She'd had enough therapy after her parents' deaths to recognize the basic psychological trick of making her reveal some hidden truth by encouraging her to talk. In this case, presumably, the truth he had in mind was her secret wish to be talked out of having a baby.

"Yes, it does," she said. "I'm willing to discuss this with you and reassure you and the clinic that I'm a good candidate, but it seems to me that in order for this to work, you must be impartial. To insure that I'm committed to the child's welfare, not to waste valuable time—yours *and* mine—trying to talk me out of my decision."

"Are you afraid I *will* talk you out of it?"

"Not at all." She tried to maintain her calm. "Look, as you are aware, the timing of this treatment relies on…" She searched for a delicate way to put it. "…my monthly cycle. I'm afraid that we will waste so much time driving down this dead-end road that we'll miss this month's, er, window of opportunity, that the entire process will be delayed. You've got my chart there, I assume. So you know I might need many attempts and that, even then, the chances of it working are slim. I don't want to wait. Surely you can understand that."

He looked at the chart, and his expression, when he looked back at her, was more compassionate. "I do sympathize with your concern. But surely you understand that I can't rush things simply because a patient may have trouble conceiving."

"If it's possible at all," she said, her voice wavering slightly with emotion. Stay calm, she told herself. Breathe.

"If it's possible at all," he agreed.

She took a moment to collect herself, then asked, "All right, what do I have to do to convince you?"

"Slow down a little. Truthfully, Miss Tourbier, I'm less concerned with your complete lack of experience with children than I am with your all-fired determination to do this so quickly *despite* the inexperience."

He didn't think she could do it. He wasn't even going to give her a chance. He was going to take his little notes and then recommend to the clinic that she was a bad candidate for the treatment. Her dreams for a child, or children, would be blown out like a match, on this one man's whim.

"Please, Dr. Cross," she said, her heart beginning to ache. "What can I do to prove to you that I'm ready for this?"

He tapped his pen on the paper a couple of times, then let go of it.

Melanie watched it clatter on his desk.

"I have a suggestion," he said.

Hope surged in her. He hadn't written her off yet. Not that he had the right to simply write her off.

"What is it?" she asked.

"Actually, it's more of a challenge. Or—" he lowered his chin and looked at her seriously "—you might even call it a dare."

Two

"A dare?" Melanie repeated, frowning. "Okay, I'm listening. What is it?" She looked like a gambler, waiting to see where the ball would settle on the roulette wheel.

Jared Cross sensed that this was a woman who was used to taking chances, who perhaps even relished them.

His mind strayed to the tabloid newspaper article he had in his file. His secretary had showed it to him, thinking it was cool that such a major celebrity was coming to the clinic. Jared hadn't shared her enthusiasm, particularly once he'd read the article. Granted, it was a tabloid and he took everything he read with a grain of salt, but several facts were unrefuted: one, that Miss Tourbier's lover was married, and two, that they'd behaved indiscreetly in front of the man's children.

Of course, it had been a couple of years ago, according to the article, which described a book that was coming out detailing the affair. Perhaps she'd learned something from it. Perhaps she was more responsible now, at least about what she did or did not do in front of children.

That was the kind of thing he needed to determine.

He would be fair, despite her obvious and unfounded fear that he was against her.

He leaned toward her, elbows on his desk. This plan, he knew, would benefit everyone involved. "I challenge you to volunteer for, say, two weeks in the hospital day-care center."

"Two weeks!"

He nodded.

"With ill children?" Her bravado was gone. She looked doubtful, and suddenly more vulnerable than he would have imagined possible. "Do you think I'm qualified to help out with them? I'd hate to say the wrong thing and make things worse." She gave a half smile. "I have a tendency to talk before I think. Sometimes it gets me into trouble."

He couldn't help but smile back. He felt as if this was the first thing she'd said to him since coming in that wasn't a previously devised closing argument. "No kidding."

She gave him a withering look.

"Okay, okay. Here's the deal. The day care is for the use of staff members, and sometimes the children or siblings of patients. There's nothing particularly challenging about it. Like all kids, they just need care and kindness and attention."

She still looked reluctant. "I'm sure I could handle it, but how would the parents feel about having me there? I'm sure they didn't leave their kids with the idea that just anyone could come in and work with them.''

"I'm not asking just anyone," Jared said, glad that she'd raised the issue. It showed she was thinking the right way. "I'm asking you. But if you don't think you're up to it—''

"Of course I'm up to it." She bristled at the challenge, as he knew she would. "In fact, I think it sounds like fun.''

"Good.''

"But I know what you're up to," she added, jabbing a finger toward him in the air. "This isn't a little dare, it's a test. So I want to know your criteria for passing.''

"Look, Miss Tourbier, I'm not playing games. You can't simply connect the dots and win a child.''

"Win a child?" she repeated incredulously. "Dr. Cross, even if you believe that's what I'm here to do, I would imagine you could find a less crass way to express your feelings. You're not only disparaging me, you're demeaning the child I hope to have, and I will not stand for that. Besides—" she threw her arms up "—you're the one devising this silly scheme to prove myself.''

"Miss Tourbier, I'm trying to help you, to give you a little taste of motherhood while there's still time for you to decide it's not what you want at this time." He saw her objection coming and raised a hand. "*If* there's even the possibility that you might decide that. I know you say there isn't. If that's so, then this is just a little practice for the real thing. No harm, no foul.''

She looked at him with narrowed eyes. "Tell me, do you make every prospective mother jump through these kinds of hoops? Is this how the hospital gets volunteers?"

He was quiet for a moment. "Every case is different. I don't make this particular suggestion to everyone, although everyone does undergo a waiting period with counseling to make sure they're making the right decision. Not every clinic does that. But not every clinic cares the way Mission Creek does. I suspect it's our reputation for being cautious that brought you here.''

"Among other things," she agreed. "But I still feel you have a prejudice against me particularly."

"I'm not punishing you by asking you to work with the kids. I'm trying to *help* you, to allow you a taste of the real, everyday process of caring for a child. If it arms you with a little experience for your future child, I've done you a favor. If it gives you pause and causes you to wait on your plan, then I've done you *and* the child a favor.''

Melanie took a long breath, then expelled it. "That makes sense," she admitted. "I just wish I believed you were even a tiny bit open-minded about my plan."

He smiled. "I wish you were a little more open-minded about it, too."

She looked at him for a moment, her blue eyes as

light as the summer sky, but the expression in them dark. Dangerous. "This is not going to change my mind, you know."

"Maybe it will, maybe it won't." He had to admire her determination. Truth was, he had nothing against her personally. He merely knew what it was like to be an unwanted child. Fifteen years in the Drumoldry Orphanage had given him all the evidence he'd ever needed.

His birth mother had kept him for the first three years of his life. All he remembered of her was the smell of alcohol, a lot of yelling, and cockroaches crawling around the floors of the succession of cheap motels they slept in.

Oh, and the boyfriends. His mother had had a lot of them. He'd seen more than any kid should have to see.

It wasn't just his own experience that made him so protective of childrens' rights, it was the experiences of the children he'd known in Drumoldry: Mary Cassidy, whose father was unknown and whose mother lost a battle with cancer when Mary was the undesirable-to-adoptive-parents age of eleven; Bobby Miller Nordell who had come in at four years of age, then was returned at six by a couple who had managed to have their own children and didn't want him any longer; Alex Jergen, who'd been left in the orphanage parking lot at age three and who stayed with them until he gave in to his depression at fifteen.

Jared knew too many stories just like theirs.

"It's not personal," Jared repeated. "It's about the child. Please work with me on this so we can make sure we do what's best for him or her. And what's best for you. A couple of weeks isn't a long time to wait when you're talking about creating a new life."

She studied him for a moment. He didn't know what she saw there, but her expression softened suddenly. "Okay. We'll do it your way. When can I start at the day-care center?"

"How about tomorrow morning? I'll call and arrange it with them, let them know you're coming. Say, nine o'clock?"

She nodded. "I'll be there at nine sharp."

She was late.

She hadn't even opened her eyes until ten that morning. It was jet lag, of course. Melanie had never been a late sleeper and she certainly wasn't lazy, but she knew it would be hard to convince Dr. Jared Cross of that.

How many points was this going to count against her?

She scurried around the bedroom of her rented apartment in The Aldon Towers, throwing on the most conservative, June Cleaverish clothes she could find. She gave her long dark hair the quickest once-over with a brush and pulled it back into a long ponytail. Forget makeup; the kids wouldn't care. Besides, the less conspicuous she was, the better. Remarkably, no one in this little town had taken much notice of her so far. She only hoped that would continue to be the case.

She pounded out to the street where her car was parked, wondering if there was even a chance that Dr. Cross wouldn't discover she was late on her first day there.

Nah. He was probably there right now, she thought as she forced herself to keep to the twenty-five-mile-an-hour speed limit on Mission Creek Drive while the clock on the dashboard seemed to move at double speed. Ten-ten, ten-fourteen, ten-nineteen.

With luck she found a parking space in the street and hurried up the sidewalk, passing a magazine kiosk. The tabloid headline seemed to jump out and grab her by the throat: A Wild Heiress! And there was that stupid photo again—the one that managed to make it look as if she and Robert were in a very compromising position when, in fact, he had knocked into the edge of her chaise longue and fallen, or pretended to fall, right on top of her. In reality, the children had screamed with laughter at their father's "clumsiness."

In the photo, though, it looked as if the children were screaming with horror at what they'd found their father doing with Melanie.

Truth was, Melanie and Roberto had never done more than kiss, but there was no convincing the world of that. People didn't want to believe that nothing salacious had actually occurred.

It just wasn't as interesting.

Melanie ducked her head as she passed the vendor and kept a low profile as she dashed through the hospital door. Ten twenty-three.

By the time she'd asked at the information desk and followed the directions to the day-care center, it was ten twenty-eight and Melanie was out of breath from running through the maze of corridors.

The first person she saw was Dr. Jared Cross.

In fact, she ran smack into him as she entered the center.

"Oh, sorry!"

He helped her regain her footing, placing his hands on her shoulders until she'd righted herself. "Miss Tourbier," he said in a voice better suited to an elementary school principal. "What a surprise."

She couldn't fault him for being angry, even if she didn't like his attitude. "I'm so sorry I'm late. This really isn't like me, honestly. My internal clock is all out of whack at the moment. Jet lag. I couldn't get to sleep until three this morning and then I guess I slept through my alarm." She tossed her hands up and tried to catch her breath. "I'm sorry."

"You have trouble when you don't get enough sleep?" he asked.

Oh, give it a rest, she wanted to say. "No more than anyone else. I swear I'm never late for things," she said, damning her luck. "This is very unusual for me."

Before he could give her the kind of superior response she could see was coming, they were interrupted by a buxom woman in her midsixties, with pale hair piled atop her head.

"Dr. Cross, is this the young woman you told me about?"

"Yes, Emily, this is Melanie Tourbier. Melanie, this is Ms. Woods, the day-care director."

"Call me Em," she said, extending her hand and smiling warmly. "We don't stand much on formality here."

"Em, I'm so glad to meet you." Melanie tried to ignore the chill from the icy Jared Cross next to her. "As I was explaining to Dr. Cross, I've just flown in from London—"

"And are your arms tired?" Em finished with a laugh. "I apologize. That kind of joke goes over big around here. You might as well get used to it. As for your being late, I'm aware that you've come from overseas and am frankly impressed that you were able to get yourself together as early as you did. Jet lag can be ferocious."

Melanie's shoulders sagged in relief. "I won't be late again," she promised sincerely.

"Please don't fret about it." Em lowered her voice for a moment before she added, "I have to say, you're even more beautiful in person than you are in your pictures."

Melanie thought of the pictures the woman might be referring to and blushed.

Em continued, "I saw photos in *House and Home* from a party you gave for the king of Jordan."

"Oh," Melanie breathed. "Yes, I remember those."

"It looked so lovely. I hope our humble hospital doesn't seem too dull to you."

Jared cleared his throat.

Melanie ignored him. "So far, it's been a real treat to be here. *Almost* everyone has been so kind and gracious."

"Almost everyone here is like that," Jared interjected. "Isn't that right, Em?"

"Yes, indeed. And, Melanie, we're so glad to have you here. It was awfully good of Dr. Cross to suggest it."

Melanie turned guilelessly to the doctor. "Yes, wasn't it?"

His mouth cocked into the smallest smile, and Melanie could have sworn she saw a moment of laughter in his eyes. "I can the see two of you are going to do just fine together. So if you'll excuse me, I have appointments." He leveled a sea-green gaze on Melanie. "I'll come back and check on you later."

Something shivered through her and made her heart pump faster when he looked at her. "That won't be necessary."

"I think it's best."

"I'm not surprised."

"In the meantime, if you need to get in touch with me, you can call through the hospital operator. They'll know how to find me."

She wondered if he was hoping she'd call him in

half an hour and tell him she'd changed her mind about everything. Well, that wasn't going to happen. "I'll be fine. So will the children. I promise that at the end of the day there will have been no fatalities."

"That's reassuring."

She watched him nod to Em and head for the door. She might have reaffirmed her decision that he was just as cold as ice, if it hadn't been for what happened right before he opened the door.

A small child, a boy with carrot-red hair, who seemed to move faster and more steadily than someone his size should, ran up and clung to Jared's legs.

"Nooo!" the child cried, clearly trying to stop Jared from leaving.

Melanie expected Jared to brush him off in a pleasant but firm manner. Instead he reached down and swooped the child into the air.

"It's a bird...it's a plane...it's Superkid!"

The child screamed with laughter.

Jared laughed, too, and Melanie's breath caught in her chest. The laugh completely transformed his face. He had dimples for one thing, not childlike little dents but manly smile lines. She hadn't noticed them before, although he'd smiled politely once or twice yesterday. But not real smiles like this. His eyes crinkled at the corners, making him look as kind as a favorite grandfather.

In fact, for just one crazy moment, Melanie could see him as a grandfather many years down the road. In her mind's eye, she saw him, a little older, a little gray at the temples, reaching down in the same motion for a little boy with dark hair and green eyes....

"Okay, sport, I've gotta go," Jared said, giving the child a final toss-and-catch before placing him gently on the floor.

"Nooo!" the little boy cried again, clutching at Jared's pant leg. "Don't go, don't go, don't go! Play ba!"

Jared knelt in front of the child and took his tiny hands in his. "How about if I come back and play ball after lunch?"

The boy chewed his lip, as if considering. "Lunch?"

"*After* lunch," Jared said. "If you're a good boy till then, we'll play a little ball before I go back to work."

The child's face brightened. "I be good!"

Jared laughed. "Then I'll see you after lunch."

Em walked up behind Melanie and watched the scene with her. "That's little Johnny Souffel. Last month he turned three and still hadn't said a word. Dr. Cross has been treating him for just over four weeks and the difference, as you can see, is remarkable."

Melanie was surprised. Granted, she didn't know much about children, but she wouldn't have believed that a month ago Johnny didn't talk. "So Dr. Cross does something here other than family planning?" she asked Em.

"Oh, my, yes. Dr. Cross is the finest child psychiatrist in all of Texas. Maybe even in the whole United States.''

Melanie turned to Em. "Child psychiatrist? Are you serious?''

"Yes, indeed.''

She wanted to ask why on earth he was wasting his time and talent trying to talk people out of having children, but she didn't know Em well enough for that. "So he just volunteers at the clinic or something?''

"Oh, yes, he's done it for years. He's a fierce child-welfare advocate. He's done a lot of good work at the clinic, and arranged more than a few very successful adoptions.'' Em clucked her tongue like a proud mother hen. "The children are so lucky to have him.''

Melanie watched little Johnny go over to an older boy and hold a block out to him. "You play?'' he asked, and the older child took the block and set it on the pile he'd already arranged into a wall.

Then Johnny went over and knocked the whole thing down.

"You had a different impression of Dr. Cross, didn't you?'' Em asked gently.

Melanie began to object, but the director held up a hand and said, "A lot of people get the wrong impression when they first meet him.''

Melanie smiled. "I guess it's fair to say that I didn't think he was the kindly type when I first met him.''

Em chuckled. "I don't think I'm telling tales out

of school when I say that Dr. Cross has a more natural rapport with children than adults. But he's a good man. I like him very much.''

Although Melanie couldn't go so far as to agree with everything Em said, she nodded. "It certainly looks as if the children like him."

"There's no better gauge of character than that," Em said, then let out an alarmed exclamation and called, "Allison, Paul, we do *not* pour water on each other's heads!" She gave Melanie a quick, exasperated smile. "Excuse me. Duty calls. Why don't you get to know the children?"

But how? Melanie wanted to ask, but the director had already gone to tend to the crisis. She'd simply approach one of the kids and get started that way. It wasn't that big a deal. She'd chatted with dignitaries from all over the world; she'd been to state dinners at the White House and tea at Buckingham Palace.

Children couldn't be *that* much more intimidating.

A nurse walked in holding a small toddler. She approached Melanie and shifted the child from one hip to the other. "Hi, I'm Linda Darrow," she said. "Do you know where Em is?"

Melanie started to point to where Em had just been with Allison and Paul, but she was nowhere to be seen. "She was just here. I'm sure she'll be back in a moment."

Linda looked at her watch. "Oh, rats, I'm already late for my shift."

"Is there something I could help you with?" Melanie asked, hoping she sounded more confident than she was.

The woman frowned. "Do you work here?"

"No. Well, yes, but only temporarily. You see, I—"

"Wait a minute. You're Melanie Tourbier!" Linda gasped. She clapped a hand to her cheek. "Oh my gosh, I thought that was just a rumor!"

Melanie felt her face go hot. "You thought what was a rumor?"

"That you were here at the hospital." The nurse shook her head. "I thought you looked familiar... You don't look like your pictures."

"Pictures can be manipulated. Believe me."

"I know it," Linda said. "My husband was at the airport last month and got a picture taken that looks just like he's standing there with the President. Of course, it's just a cutout."

Melanie laughed.

"What on earth are you doing working in the nursery?" Linda asked, then lowered her voice. "Are you trying to escape the paparazzi?"

That was a fortunate by-product of being in South Texas. So far, the paparazzi didn't know she was here. With any luck, they'd concentrate on more interesting people and not even look. Although she was modest about how interesting she was to the public, Melanie was realistic enough to know that, thanks to Roberto's book, her being here to get artificially inseminated was newsworthy to the tabloids.

"Actually, Linda," she said in a confidential tone,

"I'm here for a medical procedure, but I don't really want people to know I'm here, if I can avoid it."

Linda made the sign of locking her lips and throwing away the key. "They won't hear it from me. In fact, I'll squelch the rumors if I can."

Melanie smiled. "Thanks. Now, since I am working here for the moment, what can I do for you?"

"I need to leave Dan here for a couple of hours this morning." Again she shifted her grip on the squirming toddler. "My mother normally takes him but she has a dental appointment. Em knows I have to spring this on her every once in a while, but usually I'm able to give her at least a little warning."

"No problem," Melanie said, hoping she was right and that it wasn't going to be a problem for Em. "You just leave little Dan with me and I'll see to it that he gets the very best care."

"Thanks." Linda shuffled the warm bundle to Melanie's arms without hesitation. "My mom will be here by noon. Em knows her." She glanced at her watch again and made a face. "Gotta run. It was nice meeting you, and don't worry, mum's the word!"

She rushed off, leaving Melanie standing there with the toddler in her arms, staring at her. He didn't seem afraid, merely curious. His little face, just a few inches from hers, was so cute she nearly laughed.

"Hi there," she said to him.

He blinked his large blue eyes, studying her silently.

"You want to play?" she asked.

He still didn't answer. She wondered if he understood her.

"How about if we read a book?"

At this, his eyes lit up and he smiled. "Book," he repeated, enunciating the *k*. "Book."

Melanie felt nothing short of triumphant. "Yes, book!" They were communicating. It was a great feeling. "Let's find a book."

She carried him over to a shelf of picture books and leaned over to pick one. "Oh, *Goodnight Moon*," she said, in a tone of reverence. She took the familiar favorite off the shelf and looked at the picture on the front. She hadn't seen it in at least twenty years and probably longer, but she knew every tiny detail right down to the number of stars out the window.

One of the clearest memories she had of her mother was of her reading *Goodnight Moon* to her when she was small. "And goodnight to the old lady whispering 'hush'..."

She carried the book and the child to a large comfortable rocking chair and sat down to read. The boy settled in against her, his blond head warm against her chest.

Melanie smiled down at the top of his head, then opened the book. "'In the great green room,'" she started, then stopped for a moment, trying to swallow the lump in her throat.

The boy turned in her lap and touched her chin.

She reached up and twined the little fingers in hers.

"'There was a telephone and a red balloon and a picture of the cow jumping over the moon.'"

The boy pointed a pudgy little finger and moved it across the next page to the picture of the little mouse. Melanie laughed with sheer delight, remembering how she used to do that same thing herself. Find the mouse in every color picture. She supposed it was something all parents passed on to their children.

He moved his finger to the picture of the window. "Star," he said, pointing at the little white specks.

"That's right, stars."

She read the rest of the book, stopping to linger over the pictures on every page. It gave her a funny feeling to see them again. In a way, it made her melancholy, remembering the warmth of her childhood, and then the sudden cold when she'd lost her parents. But it also lit within her an optimism that she could feel that warmth again, with her own child. The fire would be rekindled and she would keep it stoked this time.

She finished the book and closed it. "Should we read another one?" she asked Dan, setting the book aside.

"Book," he said, but he stayed where he was, leaning comfortably against her. She loved the feeling so much she didn't want to move.

He tipped his head back and pointed to her ear. "Star," he said.

"Ear," she corrected.

Dan was insistent. "Star." He touched her diamond stud earring.

"Oh, I see. It looks like a star, yes."

"Star," he said again, nodding and pushing his finger against it.

"Hey, Dan," a familiar voice said next to them. "Melanie. How's it going?"

Melanie looked up, surprised to see Jared Cross again. Was he checking up on her already? He'd only been gone for about twenty minutes. "Fine," she said in a clipped voice.

"Good."

"Did you come back hoping I'd given up?" she asked, certain that he'd done exactly that.

"Star," Dan said again.

"That's right, honey, star," she said, hoping Jared would notice the instant rapport she had with the child, the ease with which she dealt with him. "Well?" she asked Jared in a low tone.

He was looking at her strangely. Or so she thought. "What are you doing there, Dan?" he asked.

"He's looking at my earring," Melanie told him. "We just read a book and talked about the stars in it and now he's telling me that my earring looks like a star." She looked at Jared steadily. "Everything is under control."

He frowned. "You're not wearing an earring."

"What do you mean I'm not wearing an earring? Yes, I am. Right here." She lifted her hand to her ear and felt for it.

It was gone.

She looked at Dan, just as he raised his pinched finger and thumb to his mouth. The diamond caught the light for an instant and flashed.

"Oh, my God, Dan, *no*," she said, panicked.

Unfortunately, the child also panicked at the tone of her voice and he jerked his hand into his mouth.

Melanie saw it just as it went in. *"No!"*

The child began to cry.

The blood drained into Melanie's toes. "Dan, honey." She tried to sound calm but she could clearly hear the mounting hysteria in her voice. "Let me have that back. Open your mouth, honey."

The baby stopped wailing and poked his lip out, still sniffling softly.

"What's going on?" Jared asked, leaning down. "What's he got?"

"My earring," she said a little shrilly. "A diamond earring."

"He's got your earring in his mouth?" Jared bent down to try to get it out.

She poked her finger into the child's mouth and felt around. Nothing. "No," she said, pulling a shaking hand back and looking at Jared in terror. "Not anymore. He swallowed it."

Three

"He swallowed it?" Jared picked the child up from Melanie's lap. He was still calm, but there was an undercurrent in his voice.

She nodded, kneading her hands in front of her. "One-carat diamond stud. Oh, my God, what am I going to do?"

He gave her an impatient glance before turning his attention back to the child. "I'm sure your insurance will cover it."

His words didn't compute. "Insurance?"

He set the child on top of a table and told him to open wide. "Yes," he said into Dan's mouth, poking around with his finger. "You can get yourself a new— What did you say it was? One carat diamond?"

Melanie understood his implication. "I'm not worried about the diamond," she said, drawing herself up. "I'm worried about the *b-o-y.*"

Dan looked at her with wide blue eyes. Oh, no, could he spell? She didn't want to alarm him any more than necessary.

"The earring wasn't huge," she continued in a very soothing tone, with half an eye toward Dan, "but it wasn't exactly a strawberry seed, either.'' She took the other earring out of her ear and showed it to Jared. ''It was this size. Can this hurt him?''

Jared took the earring and examined it. ''It's a short post, that's good.''

She nodded eagerly. ''I have them made that way because I don't like getting poked when I sleep.''

He gave her a puzzled look.

''By the post, I mean,'' she explained. ''They're sharp.''

''I see.''

Silence hung between them.

''I swallowed an ice cube once,'' Melanie said, trying to reassure herself more than to inform him. ''It was a lot bigger than that and it went down. Of course, I was older and it melted eventually, but still... Maybe this will go right through him, right?''

''Hopefully.''

Em came into the room from the kitchen area, with two children with wet hair. ''Is something wrong?'' she asked, her brow furrowed.

''It's my fault,'' Melanie said quickly. It was all she could do not to throw herself into Em's arms, sobbing. ''Dan was fiddling with my earring and I startled him and he—he swallowed it!''

''Your earring? How big was it?''

Melanie held the other one out to Em in a hand that trembled. ''It was like this.''

''Oh, thank goodness it wasn't a big one.''

Melanie was somewhat relieved. ''It seems big

when you think of it going through that little digestive system.''

To Melanie's surprise, Em patted her arm kindly. ''These things happen. Quite a lot around here, as a matter of fact. What do you think, Dr. Cross?'' There was concern in her eyes, but at least she didn't look alarmed.

''He needs to go upstairs for an X ray,'' Jared said.

''An X ray?'' Melanie's knees felt weak. Oh, no. This was bad. This was very, very bad.

Em put a hand on her shoulder. ''Now, now. It's just a formality, to make sure it's not stuck someplace it shouldn't be. We always have to have an X ray, then we just let nature take its course.''

''I'll call up there and tell them he's coming,'' Jared said briskly, going to the small office in the next room.

Melanie nodded and took the child back into her arms. Immediately he leaned his head against her chest. A sob caught in her throat, and she laid her cheek against his feathery-soft blond curls. ''I'm sorry, baby. You feel okay?''

He didn't answer, but she didn't expect him to.

''Why don't you take him to the X-ray department on the seventh floor now?'' Em suggested. ''I can hold down the fort here.''

''Do you really trust me to do that?'' Melanie asked, worried that Em had forgotten who'd caused all this trouble in the first place.

''Why, of course.'' Em looked surprised.

"Thank you." Melanie's words came out in a rush of gratitude. "I won't let you down."

"Melanie, dear, it was a mistake. Please don't beat yourself up about it. Just let them check Dan out, then call Linda on the hospital phone and let her know what happened."

Melanie nodded. "I will, absolutely."

When Jared came back he said, "They're waiting. I'll take you up there. I have to pick up a chart from the seventh floor anyway." He turned to Em. "Is Lily Palmer ready? I came down to get her for an appointment."

"She certainly is." Em called a child of about six over to join them.

Melanie was glad that Em and Jared were not so worried about Dan that they couldn't think about anything else. That had to be a good sign.

"Dr. Cross!" the little girl squealed when she saw him. "Are we going to talk about my baby brother again?"

He smiled at her. "If you like."

They all began walking toward the door.

"Whatever." The child flipped her hair. "I'm not so sad about him coming anymore. Mommy said she'd hire me to help her when he's here, but I don't have to change smelly old diapers!"

"Sounds like you got a good deal," he said, and the child laughed and ran ahead.

"Is she a patient of yours?" Melanie asked, holding Dan close as they rounded the corner to the elevators.

"A temporary one," he answered. "Fortunately her problems were not very serious. Her mom's a doctor here and due to give birth next month. Lily's been having a little trouble with jealousy."

"Oh, she'll probably be thrilled when the baby comes along," Melanie said. "Who wouldn't be?"

Jared shot her a look, but smiled. "I'm sure she will. And your point is taken."

Melanie feigned innocence. "My point?"

"Press the button," Jared said to Lily, who proceeded to press it about ten times in rapid succession. "Yes, your point," he said to Melanie. "How are you enjoying working with the kids?"

"Piece of cake," she said.

He looked from her to Dan and back again, clearly trying not to smile. "That so?" The elevator arrived and they stepped on.

Her face grew warm. "Okay, maybe it's not quite as easy as I thought it would be. But you have to admit working in day care is very different from having a child of one's own."

"We'll see."

We'll see? Her heart lurched. Did that mean he was going to give her the okay? She knew better than to ask. Instead she just nodded. "I feel as confident as I ever did. Maybe even more."

He raised an eyebrow. "More?"

"Sure. Look, already today I've learned that you

can feed babies rocks and metal and they can, hope-fully, just poop it out.''

Jared watched the digital numbers change over the door as the elevator went up. Although he didn't ex-actly smile, she recognized a lightening of his ex-pression. "That should come in handy if you should ever go broke."

There it was again. Was he hinting to her that he was going to approve her as an artificial insemination candidate?

The doors opened and they stepped out.

"Luckily my parents left me with enough to pro-vide for my children," she said. "I don't think we'll have to resort to eating the elements, but it's good to know that we can."

To her amazement, he laughed. "You're resource-ful, I'll give you that." They stopped. "X-ray is down that hall and to the left. You can't miss it. They're expecting you."

"Thanks," Melanie said, thanking him as much for easing up on her as for giving her directions.

"Sure. Come on, Lily," he said. "We're going to pick something up then go to my office." He reached his hand out to the little girl, and she took it. Some-thing in the gesture made Melanie's heart ache. She watched them walk away for a moment before fol-lowing his directions to the X-ray department.

Everything went smoothly, although the waiting took longer and was more nerve-racking than Melanie had anticipated. When they finally took Dan in, they allowed Melanie to come with him. Part of her felt she didn't have the right to be there, that she should have called his mother for this, but Em had specifically told her to call Linda afterward, when everything was all right. And Em had been confident that everything *would* be all right, so there was probably no sense in getting Linda worried for nothing.

In the X-ray room, Dan fussed and complained at first, but he held still long enough for them to take the picture. Afterward, when Melanie took him back in her arms, he was happy again.

The technician took the film out of the machine and clipped it onto the light board to take a look. "There it is," he said, pointing to a small dark shadow in Dan's stomach. "Yum."

"Is he going to be all right?" Melanie asked fretfully.

"Looks like it," the attending doctor said. "He didn't suffer from any gagging or choking on its way down, so it didn't get lodged in his windpipe. The rest is pretty easy. With any luck it should come out painlessly."

Melanie sighed in relief.

"Is he going to be here in the hospital for the rest of the day?" the doctor asked.

"No, his grandmother is supposed to pick him up in about half an hour."

"See if you can keep him in the day care instead. You're going to have to watch for the earring to come out. If it hasn't by the end of the day, we might do another X ray."

Melanie swallowed. "All right. How will I know when it's come out?"

The doctor smiled. "I'm afraid you're going to have to inspect the contents of his diaper."

She tried not to appear appalled by the notion, and nodded mutely.

Next she had to call Linda Darrow and tell her what happened. She screwed up her courage and went to the white house phone on the wall. The minutes seemed to tick by extra slowly while she waited for the operator to page Linda.

Finally Linda picked up the line and, with great trepidation, Melanie told her what had happened.

When she finished, Linda sighed heavily. "I can't believe this."

"I know," Melanie said miserably. "I'm just so sorry about it."

"How much is it going to cost?"

"Whatever it is, obviously I'll cover it," Melanie said, glad she could at least do that much.

There was a pause, then Linda asked. "I'm sorry, what do you mean you'll cover it?"

"The medical costs, time you take off from work, anything."

"I meant the diamond," Linda said. "How much will it cost me to replace it for you?"

Melanie couldn't believe her ears. "You're not worried about Dan?"

"You just told me he was all right, didn't you?"
Linda asked. "We see this kind of thing, and much
worse, all the time around here. Last week we had a
girl in the ER who had swallowed one of those little
lightbulbs. *That* was harrowing."

Melanie gasped. "Was she all right?"

"Oh, sure. They got it out easy. Now about this
earring, I don't think I can buy a new one outright,
but maybe if the jeweler has some kind of installment
plan—"

"Please, Linda, no. I don't care about that at all.
The important thing is that Dan's okay." Knowing
Linda's objection was coming, she added, "I really
have to insist."

"I appreciate that, Miss Tourbier—"

"Melanie, please."

"Melanie, then. Now I'd better call Mom and tell
her not to come, then I'll come down to see Dan in
the day care as soon as I can get away."

"I'll hold on to him until you get there."

Linda clicked her tongue against her teeth. "You're
just the sweetest thing. I hope you stay in Mission
Creek for a good long time."

I hope it doesn't take a good long time for Jared
Cross to decide I can be a mother, Melanie thought,
but she said, "I hope so, too."

By the time she got back to the day-care center,
the lights were dimmed and most of the children were
sleeping on mats on the floor. Em hurried over to
Melanie and Dan and said in a hushed voice, "It's

nap time. Every day after lunch.'' She gave Melanie a sympathetic smile. ''Speaking of which, you must be starving. Why don't you give Dan to me and I'll rock him to sleep while you go grab a bite.''

The last thing Melanie was concerned with right now was food. ''May I rock him myself?'' she asked, reluctant to give up the warm little boy who seemed to like being in her arms as much as she liked having him there. ''Please?''

Em raised her eyebrows and gestured toward the chair. ''Be my guest. If you're sure.''

Melanie gave the boy a squeeze and said, ''I'm sure.'' She carried him over to the chair and sat down, settling his head in the crook of her arm. He wriggled impatiently at first, but she shushed him and quietly began singing lullabies. Within five minutes he was asleep.

And she was more positive than ever that she wanted a child of her own. No matter what it took.

Unfortunately, it looked like it would take a lot.

Jared sat by himself in the doctors lounge and ate the peanut butter and jelly sandwich he'd brought. This particular lunch was a habit he'd had for a long time.

He took a sip of the milk he'd picked up in the cafeteria and looked at the small color TV that some-one had left on in the corner.

There was some kind of news conference going on outside the Stop n' Save. A painfully thin, pale woman was talking. There were several microphones in front of her, and she was looking into the camera. Her face might have been called pixie-ish if it didn't look so hard. The caption under her read, Deena Hines, Wife of Escaped Convict Branson Hines.

"Branson," she said, her voice as thin and reedy as her body. "Please, please, come home, darlin'. I'm worried about you because I don't know where you are or how you're doin'. Please get in touch with me—" she looked slyly left and right "—or with the police." Jared thought he saw the smallest smirk curl the left side of her mouth. "Please, darlin', I want you back home. It'll be better for you if you turn yourself in, rather than letting them find you, because they are looking." At this, she broke down into strangely tearless sobs, and covered her face with her bony hands.

Jared took his trash to the can and then clicked the TV off with disgust. This was a heck of a world they lived in now. A heck of a place to raise kids. Crime had become entertainment. It was obvious from that woman's body language that she'd learned to make the television plea from all the crime victims or families of criminals who had made television pleas before her. It was as if it was all a big game.

It was easy to say that the world was too hard a place for kids now, but he knew that wasn't true. In fact, what the world needed was more good kids. More good parents having kids and raising them responsibly, into moral people.

That made him think of Melanie Tourbier. What kind of parent would she be? Her concern for little Dan Darrow had been real, but Jared didn't know how much of that concern had to do with the possibility of a lawsuit. Someone in her position probably had to think about that a lot.

He thought of the book that was coming out about her, and the tabloid headlines. He hadn't heard anything about a lawsuit over either one of those things. Did that mean the story was true?

Of course, she had every right to conduct her life however she saw fit. It wasn't as if a woman had to limit her life to *only* motherhood once she had children. Despite his own experience, Jared realized that wasn't realistic, or even healthy.

But it also wasn't healthy for a child to have to compete for attention with his mother's dates.

The trick with Melanie was going to be in determining what was most important to her, and perhaps helping her see it, too. If dating was a high priority, then maybe Jared could get her to put her parenting plans on hold. If she was gun-shy about dating, maybe he could even help her with that too somehow. To make sure she focused her need for love where it was most appropriate.

Five days later, a Monday morning, in his next session with Melanie, he decided to broach the subject.

"How have things been working out at the day-care center?" he asked her, although he knew. Em had said Melanie showed up for work early every day and insisted on staying until every child had been picked up. She had become an instant favorite among the children, even those who were normally leery of strangers and who kept to themselves.

Melanie Tourbier, according to Em, was a natural with kids.

But Jared still had his concerns.

"I've really enjoyed it," she said with a wide, genuine smile. "Though you were right about one thing. It is a little more—how do I put this?—gritty at times than I'd expected."

"How do you mean?"

She took a sip of coffee and set it down deliberately. "For instance, on my first day there, I really really enjoyed rocking little Dan Darrow and reading to him. And, of course, feeding him my jewelry," she added for levity.

Jared raised an eyebrow and tried not to smile.

"But sifting through the contents of his diaper was another thing," she went on.

Jared tried to imagine the delicate and refined Melanie Tourbier going through a soiled diaper. It almost made him laugh, but he maintained his professional composure. "That's the way it is with kids."

"I'm prepared for that," she said pointedly. "It doesn't mean I'm going to enjoy those times."

"Were you able to find the earring?"

"Oh yeah." She laughed. "But naturally it wasn't

the first thing out. Anyway, I had it cleaned up and sent to his mother with the other one.''

Jared had seen the earrings. They had to be worth thousands. "That was very generous of you.''

Melanie's cheeks glowed pink. "Nonsense. It was nothing. I felt it was the very least I could do, considering the worry Linda must have gone through.'' She got a faraway look. "I think that must be the most difficult part of parenting. The worry.''

He thought for a moment. "Good point. We've talked about how difficult the work of having a child can be when you're a single parent, but we haven't talked about other concerns that are specific to the single parent.''

She frowned. "Such as?''

"Your social life." He eyed her steadily.

Her face grew a shade paler, but she didn't move. Her hands remained folded primly in her lap. "What about it?''

He stepped carefully through what he suspected was an emotional minefield. "It's difficult enough for couples to have a social life after they've had a child, but for a single person it's very difficult to juggle parenthood with dating, not to mention the effects of dating on the child.''

She looked relieved. "Oh, well, I'm not dating, so I don't think that will be a problem for me.''

"But it's no secret that you've had an active social life.'' He watched her for a reaction, but she didn't give him one. "How will you fit a baby in?''

She considered his question for a moment. "For one thing, I imagine I'll be spending more time in parks and museums and less at state dinners." She smiled. "Wow, that benefit didn't even occur to me before. I'll have the perfect excuse to stay home."

Jared could think of a dozen people who would have given their limbs to take her place at state dinners, though for him the lifestyle held no allure.

It was interesting that Melanie shared his opinion.

He made an unimportant note on his pad and asked, "What if you should meet someone and want to start a relationship?" He doodled a spiral.

She laughed. "Don't tell me—you have a friend who would be just perfect for me, right?"

Jared's pen stopped moving and he looked at her, surprised. "I beg your pardon?"

Melanie waved a hand. "Never mind, I'm just joking. Everyone seems to want to set me up on a blind date."

"Really?" He resumed the spiral. It got very dark.

"Yes. In fact, I probably get offers at least once a week. Someone's cousin or nephew or neighbor's brother's grandson." She sighed.

Jared wondered what it would be like—for those cousins, nephews or grandsons—to go on a date with Melanie Tourbier. It was probably enjoyable, he thought. Men liked women like this; pretty women, with dancing eyes and gleaming hair, who smelled of sweet perfume and who were always ready to laugh.

Yes, she probably had plenty of guys ready to jump when she told them how high and where to land.

It was a pity none of them had worked out. If they had, she probably wouldn't be here right now, trying to start a family on her own.

Melanie continued, unaware of the turn Jared's thoughts had taken. "It seems like the rest of the world is a lot more uncomfortable with my being single than I am," she said.

"Why is that, do you think?" He knew why. Because she didn't come across as a loner. For one thing, she radiated sensuality. Whether she knew it or not, she created the impression that, if she didn't *need* a man, she was certainly equipped to make one happy.

She met his eyes and shrugged. "I don't know. Either they think I'm not capable of taking care of myself, or all the world's a matchmaker. I think it's the latter." She smiled. "You're single, aren't you? You probably get the same thing from your friends. That's just how people are."

Jared had had his share of setups, but he just didn't have time for that kind of frivolity. "Do you accept any of those offers?" he asked, noticing a slight edge in his voice.

She folded her hands in her lap and grew serious again. "Not really. I'm very cautious about that kind of thing. With a baby in my life, I would be even more careful. The baby would come first."

He nodded. She was giving the right answers, but

then it didn't take a genius to know what the right answers were.

What he wanted was her explanation for the scandal the tabloids were focused on right now, and some kind of reassurance that the headlines didn't really reflect the woman's character. He wanted to know that she wouldn't have a long series of "uncles" for the child and, perhaps even more importantly, that there weren't more scandals in the future that might affect or embarrass the poor kid.

"And what about when the child is older?" Jared asked, as gently as he could. He started doodling again. "In some ways, it's easier to parent a baby, because the choices you make are those of survival. As the child gets older, there are more—" the pen tore through the paper and he stopped "—moral considerations."

She looked thoughtful. "I'm not sure what you're getting at. Surely there are moral considerations all along the way. Every family has its own set of standards. I certainly will."

She'd tossed the ball in the air so he grabbed it. "Exactly." He set the pen down and leaned back in his chair. "What are your standards, Miss Tourbier? For example, what about—" he pretended to ruminate "—sex?"

She looked at him narrowly. She was suspicious of him.

Perhaps she was right to be. Should he really have been so blunt? Why was he finding it so difficult to talk to her? He did this all the time, it was his job, for Pete's sake. He'd never had trouble talking to a patient before. It was as if he had to be more careful with Melanie Tourbier than with most people, even though it was her life he was talking to her about. Her lifestyle he was concerned about.

"Dr. Cross, I must be misunderstanding you. I'm sure you're not asking for details about my private sex life."

He chose his words carefully. "Not per se. But a certain amount of detail about your private life is relevant to our counseling."

She raised her chin. Her blue eyes burned with controlled defiance. "Not this kind of detail," she said sharply. "I find it extremely difficult to believe that you'd question anyone else this way."

"I would if, in my professional opinion, I felt it was necessary."

"Really? What if a married couple came in for counseling? Would you be asking them for salacious details about their private life?"

"No, but I'm not asking you for salacious details, either."

"Would you ask them for any details about their sex lives?"

"Probably not, but—"

"So what's the difference? You don't know what they do behind closed doors. They could swap wives with the neighbors every Friday night after a game of bridge."

He tried not to laugh. "I seriously doubt any of the couples I've counseled do that."

"But you don't *know*," Melanie argued. "You never know about people. Sometimes you just have to take it on faith that they're good, upstanding citizens who wouldn't expose children to inappropriate behavior."

"I have to follow my instincts," he told her evenly.

She looked hurt. "Do your instincts tell you that I'm some sort of sexual deviate?"

Actually, his instincts told him that she was a warm-blooded woman who could and probably did drive a lot of men wild with desire. Even Jared, who had his professional veneer on pretty securely, felt himself reacting to her once in a while as a man instead of as a therapist.

But, no, he didn't believe she was a sexual deviate.

"Well, Dr. Cross?" she demanded.

"I'm not accusing you of anything heinous, Miss Tourbier," he said. "Please listen to me. All I'm doing is what I'm paid to do—counsel you and ensure that you are prepared to become a parent. My job is the same whether it's for a single woman like yourself or a married couple. But as lifestyles differ, so do my questions. And my questions to you are the same I would ask any young, vibrant, single woman who is used to living on her own and taking care of herself. Now—" he looked at his watch "—I see that our time is up for today."

"Do you always get the last word?"

He gave a half smile. "Do you want it?"

"I'd just like to finish this particular conversation."

"I believe you have an appointment on Wednesday, as well, so we can continue this discussion then."

She gave him a heated glare. "I'd like to finish it now, Doctor, so we don't have to revisit it."

He would, too, but he had a young patient coming in five minutes. "I'm sorry, but I have another appointment." He closed her folder and set it aside, picking up the folder for his next patient in a pointed way.

"Then I'll wait."

He stopped his paper shuffling. "I beg your pardon?"

"I'll wait until you're free. Surely you don't have appointments stacked up all day and night."

He set the folder down and looked at Melanie. "Don't you have to get back to the day-care center?"

Her face flushed pink. "Oh. Yes, I guess I do."

He let out a breath. "Look, stop at my secretary's desk and find out if I've had any cancellations before our next meeting. If so, we can meet sooner and hash this out."

"I'll do that," Melanie declared, collecting herself and standing up. "But I have to tell you, Dr. Cross, I'll also be making an appointment with the hospital administrator. I'd like to talk to her about your methods of counseling."

Four

Melanie took a moment to gather control before she pasted on her most charming smile and went to Dr. Cross's secretary, Wendy.

"Can I help you?" the woman asked. Today her curly bright-red hair was pulled back in an obvious effort to tame the curls, but several unruly strands framed her face. "Oh, Miss Tourbier! How are you?"

"Great, Wendy," Melanie lied. "Listen, Dr. Cross said he'd like to see me again as soon as possible. He has another patient so he asked me to check with you and see if we couldn't work something out."

"Well, sure. Let's just take a look." The woman frowned and glanced through the black bound appointment book. "He's really booked. Did he want you to take a lunch appointment?"

He hadn't said anything of the sort. But Dr. Cross wasn't being questioned now; Melanie was, and if she misunderstood Wendy's question, well, who could blame her?

"That would be fine," Melanie said. "Lunch today?"

Wendy looked uncertain. "I guess. If he said so."

"He very specifically told me to stop and talk to

you about setting up another appointment,'' Melanie said honestly.

''Okay, then.'' She scribbled Melanie's name into the slot that had an *X* through it from noon to one. ''You got it.''

''Thanks,'' Melanie said, already steeling herself for the remainder of the battle to come. ''I really appreciate it.''

Next on Melanie's list was a visit with Tabitha Monroe, the hospital administrator.

A bright woman, of medium height, with wavy dark-blond hair and blue eyes that were as sharp as they were kind, Tabitha reminded Melanie of a young, unbleached Marilyn Monroe. Melanie felt an immediate bond with her.

''Get comfortable,'' Tabitha said, indicating an oversize guest chair. ''Tell me what's going on.''

Melanie sat, noticing the proliferation of bonsai trees on the credenza behind Tabitha, and the small dragon statue on her desk. The Eastern theme helped Melanie feel at ease.

''Well, I just don't think my counseling sessions with Dr. Cross are productive. We don't get along at all.''

''I know Dr. Cross has a bit of a cool exterior,'' Tabitha understated, ''but he's truly a fine doctor and a fine man. We've never had any complaints about his job performance.''

''Until I came along, huh?'' Melanie gave an apologetic smile.

"Melanie, you are far from the first person to notice that Jared is a tough nut, but underneath it all he's a softie."

"If you'll forgive me, I find that very hard to believe," Melanie said.

"He's fiercely protective of children. I suppose you could call that his major fault, although I myself have a hard time calling that a fault. Sometimes, in his conviction, he comes across as a little too gruff."

"Or a *lot* too gruff. I've never had such shouting matches in my life."

"Really." Tabitha considered her for a moment. "That surprises me."

"It surprised me, too. Believe me, when I came here, I thought it was for fertility treatments not verbal sparring with an arrogant doctor."

Tabitha laughed. "I don't imagine anyone anticipates that when they come in for fertility treatments. But for what it's worth, I've never known him to stay on a case where there's a real personality conflict."

"He doesn't seem like a quitter to me," Melanie said.

"No, not a quitter—a good psychiatrist. He knows when a conflict is going to get in the way of his job and do the patient more harm than good."

Melanie gave a derisive snort. "We'll see about that. Honestly, he's the most infuriating man I've ever met in my life."

"He can be socially awkward at times."

"This is way beyond socially awkward. I think he hates me."

"I'm certain that's not true."

"How can you say that when all we do is bicker?"

Tabitha tapped her pen thoughtfully against her chin. "Conflict for Jared Cross doesn't usually mean argument. It doesn't usually go that far. To tell you the truth, I find it very interesting that he hasn't passed your case along, under the circumstances."

"I guess I'm just lucky."

"Or something," Tabitha said cryptically.

"What are you getting at?"

Tabitha hesitated, then expelled a long breath and said, "What do we tell little girls when little boys on the playground pull their hair and pinch them?"

Melanie saw immediately what Tabitha was getting at. "Uh-uh." She shook her head. "Dr. Cross is not pulling my metaphorical hair or pinching my metaphorical bottom because he's got some sort of schoolboy crush."

"Why do you think he's giving you such a hard time, then?"

"I think he's trying to stop me from having a baby because he thinks I won't be a good enough mother. He's prejudiced against me."

Tabitha smiled. "Let's just see what happens, okay? I won't let him make an unfair decision in your case and I'm sure you'll keep your metaphorical bottom covered."

Melanie laughed. "All right."

"If, after a couple of weeks, you still feel this isn't working, come on back and see me. We'll work it out. Unless…" She hesitated. "I do have to ask you this. Do you want to file an official grievance?"

Melanie didn't even have to think about it. "No. He's not that bad. I guess I just needed to vent. I'm sure you're right, and Dr. Cross will come to a fair decision."

Besides, she thought as she left Tabitha's office, it would certainly be faster convincing Jared Cross that she was good mother material, than having him removed from the case and having to start from the beginning with someone else.

Especially if—heaven forbid—that someone else had a similar, or even a worse, prejudice against Melanie. Normally she wouldn't think that way, but things had been pretty unpredictable since she got to Mission Creek.

She went back to the day-care center and had a wonderful time playing with the children until eleven forty-five. Then she told Em about her appointment and went back to Jared's office.

She arrived just as Wendy was packing up.

"Did you tell Dr. Cross about our appointment?" Melanie asked, expecting a heated reply from the woman who had, unfortunately, gotten into the middle of her squabble with Dr. Cross.

But Wendy was just as bubbly as ever. "I forgot," she confessed with a giggle. "Not to worry, though, I just had him paged to his office and I put your chart on his desk. Why don't you just wait in there for him?''

''Sure, but what if he doesn't show up?''

''If he's not here in ten minutes just have him paged again. But that won't be necessary. He always goes to the same break room for the same lunch at the same time every day.'' She shook her head and laughed. ''He's funny that way. Anyway, I'm positive they didn't have any trouble finding him at all. I'm off to lunch myself now, so why don't you go ahead and wait in his office?''

Melanie followed the secretary's instruction and let herself into the quiet, masculine office.

It was strange being in there without him, she thought. Almost eerie. Like all the life was gone from it. Since Jared Cross wasn't a man who exuded much obvious warmth, at least as far as Melanie was concerned, she was surprised at the absence of it without him there.

She walked around, looking idly at the shelves while she waited.

There were lots of little crafts strewn about, obviously made for him by the children who were his patients. A scrapbook on the end table by the couch held a multitude of brightly crayoned pictures done on construction paper. Most of them were inscribed to ''Dr. Cros'' or ''Dr. Kros'' and signed in broad scrawls. At least half said ''thank you,'' and the faces in all of them—whether they were faces of children, animals or, in one or two cases, houses—were smiling.

Looking through the pictures, she was glad she hadn't filed a formal complaint against him. That wasn't to say she wasn't still displeased with the way he was handling her case. But clearly there were a lot of children out there who depended on Dr. Cross and who had gotten valuable help from him. She didn't want to cause trouble for him that might result in his not being available to his young patients.

Instead she had to simply reaffirm her resolve to change his mind about her. She'd have to remain calm and help him see things logically. They'd work together and they'd both win.

She went to the chair opposite the large oak desk and sat down where she usually did. She checked her watch. It was five minutes past noon. If his secretary was right, and Dr. Cross could be easily found and summoned, he should be here any minute. She leaned back in the chair and tapped her fingers against the armrests, waiting.

That was when she noticed her chart on the top of his desk.

The chart he'd been keeping his own notes on her in.

She leaned forward and took the folder, which was clearly marked Confidential, then paused.

Was this wrong?

Of course not, she told herself. The information in the folder was confidential only to outsiders. Not to her. Heck, it was more *her* business than the doctor's, when you came right down to it.

Melanie opened the folder and started sifting through the papers. First was the usual medical history she'd expected, including the report from her doctor in London, Dr. Meikeljohn, detailing her fertility problems and proclaiming her an excellent candidate for fertility treatments. He added his opinion that she would be a spectacular parent.

The next page contained Dr. Cross's notes. This felt a little more like invasion of privacy, and Melanie hesitated over them. It felt like reading someone's diary or eavesdropping. If she wanted an explanation for something he wrote, she'd have to admit she'd been riffling through the file.

Not that there was anything wrong with that.

Still, maybe it would be better for her to leave well enough alone. Dr. Cross would be here any moment, and she could ask him point-blank what his opinion was.

She closed the folder and was about to set it back on his desk when something fell to the floor. It was a newspaper article.

Melanie bent down to pick it up. As soon as she touched it, she knew what it was. She turned it over with trembling hands. When she saw the picture, her heart sank. It was the photo of her with Roberto and his children. The photo the tabloids had published in order to sell a sexy, scandalous story, even though it was far from the truth.

Yet Dr. Cross had not only read the story, he'd cut it out and put it in her file. While she sat in front of him, laying her whole self on the line for him, being more honest and open than she'd ever been with anyone in her life, he was holding on to this garbage, believing it instead of believing the truth she spoke.

Melanie was so furious that, when Jared came into the room, she didn't even bother to pretend she hadn't looked at the file.

"Is this what you're basing your questioning on?" she asked, waving the article in the air.

"What's that?" he asked, calmly closing the door behind him and walking over to his desk. She noticed he was holding what looked like a half-eaten peanut butter and jelly sandwich.

If she wasn't so enraged, she might have found that endearing.

"It's an article from, I believe, *Private Lives of People Who Aren't Able to Defend Themselves*." She slapped the paper down on his desk and held it there with a white-knuckled fist. "Recognize it?"

He looked at her with narrowed green eyes. "Yes. It was in my file."

"You mean *my* chart."

"Which is *my* file."

They glared at each other from opposite sides of the desk, like boxers waiting for the bell.

"You had no right to go through that," Jared said, his voice hard. "It's a confidential file. It says so right on the front, as I'm sure you noticed."

"Of course I noticed. However, I didn't think that meant it was to be kept confidential from me. Considering that the entire thing is about me." She took a short breath and put her hands on her hips. "And I'd say it's a lucky thing I did open it, so that I could set you straight on a few things."

"For instance?"

"For instance, that article." She jabbed a finger toward the newspaper on his desk.

Jared opened his arms expansively. "By all means, please set me straight. Tell me why I shouldn't believe my own eyes."

"Because that photo isn't what it looks like."

He made a point of looking down at the photo for a long moment before looking back at Melanie. "No?"

"No." She struggled to maintain control of her voice. The last thing in the world she wanted right now was to be shrill. She took a deep breath and looked at him with what she hoped was condescending calm instead of the outrage and fury she was feeling. "Shall I explain?"

He picked up on her tone and matched it with his own. "I'd love to hear what you have to say about it. Have a seat." He sat down and waited for her to do the same.

She didn't. "Not everyone in this world is principled, Doctor."

He looked surprised. "I'm well aware of that."

"Well, there's no greater hotbed of unprincipled

people than those who are in the business of making money off celebrity scandals.''

''You mean the photographers.''

''Yes, but not just the photographers. A lot of those rag magazines you evidently read pay a great deal of money to anyone who can give them a story. The more salacious, the better, especially if it has the potential to ruin someone.''

''I know that's true.'' He shrugged. ''But pictures are worth a thousand words.''

''Well, then, look at the picture,'' Melanie said. ''Look at it with an objective eye, not with the mind you've already made up about me.''

''Why don't you cut to the chase?''

She cleared her throat. ''Sometimes when a photo is shot at just the right moment, it can make something appear to be happening that isn't. This is lucky for those photographers but unlucky for the subjects and for anyone else who might be interested in the truth. That picture you have there is a good example, Dr. Cross. When you look at that, you see two people behaving indiscreetly in front of small children, don't you?''

''That's exactly what I see,'' he said, glancing down at the picture again.

''Do you want to know what was really happening when that photo was shot?'' Melanie asked, finding it more and more difficult to keep her voice from catching in her throat.

''If you want to tell me.''

"Roberto Loren was an unscrupulous opportunist, with a really good line. He was kind to me, or so I thought, and we spent some time together one summer. It wasn't a romantic relationship, or, at least, it wasn't a *very* romantic relationship." She felt her face go hot. She hated talking about this, justifying herself to a stranger, but she knew it was necessary. "We didn't have sex," she said bluntly.

That seemed to catch Dr. Cross off guard. He didn't exactly blush, but there was a flicker in his eyes that told her he wasn't expecting that kind of frankness from her. "Go on," he said carefully.

"Roberto knew that didn't matter. He arranged for a photographer to hide in the bushes by the pool during a week I visited him and his children—and his sister and her children, by the way—in Majorca. Then while I was giving his girls diving lessons, he came out, pretended to trip on the stonework by the pool and landed on me like you see there. The girls laughed their heads off. If you look closely, you can see that. And you can see that's surprise on my face, not the openmouthed ecstasy you no doubt assumed it was."

He didn't look at the picture again. "This is the guy who's got a book coming out, right?"

She nodded, trying not to show her still-fresh hurt and betrayal. "He's the one. And I promise you it will be more of the same, and all of it will be lies. Just like that article you have there." She sat down and folded her hands in her lap. "Now it seems to

me you have a choice, Dr. Cross. You can either continue to read the stories about me or you can talk to
me and listen to the truth.'' She paused for a moment,
then asked, ''Which will it be?''

Usually Jared felt in control of his sessions. But
Melanie Tourbier had a way of turning everything
upside down. Now was no exception. ''I always try
to draw my own conclusions from personal interac-
tion, Miss Tourbier.''

She raised an eyebrow. ''Really? Then why did
you keep that article in my folder at all?''

''Because there are a lot of ingredients in the for-
mula for determining suitability. Newspaper articles
on the potential parents are obviously relevant.''

''If they're true.''

''If they're true,'' he agreed, deciding the best
thing to do was just be direct. ''But I'll be frank with
you, Melanie. Your picture is in more than one newspaper right now, showing you in what appear to be,
er, compromising positions.''

'''Appear to' being the key words.'' She shifted
her weight and crossed her legs. ''I've just explained
how that photo came about.''

''Yes. That one. But there are others. ''Are they all
faked?'' He kept his voice low, calm. ''You've told
me there was nothing going on in this particular picture, but you didn't say anything about what you think
is acceptable behavior with children around.''

''I would have thought I'd made that clear.''

"Why don't you make it clear now?"

She gave him an icy stare. "Well, Doc, I routinely have orgies at my house, but I'll wait until the children are asleep." She laid a hand to her cheek and looked at him with mock surprise. "Is that acceptable or unacceptable behavior?"

A muscle ticked in Jared's jaw. "Listen—"

"No."

"Excuse me?"

"I said no. I will not listen to you defame my character this way. You're not asking how I would behave if I had children, you're telling me how you *think* I'd behave, and you're telling me that you disapprove." She drew in a short, harsh breath. "This is what you've been hinting at all along, isn't it? Not my friends, not dating, not my real life. Lurid tabloid headlines and sex."

Had he crossed the line? Suddenly it wasn't clear to him what he needed to know versus what he wanted to know.

Or why he wanted to know.

Melanie, meanwhile, was on a tear. "You know, I would expect much more from a good psychiatrist."

He picked up his heavy Mont Blanc pen again and tapped it on the desk in front of him, racheting up his calm with every tap. "A good psychiatrist evaluates *all* of the facts," he said. "Not just those the patient presents."

She glared at him.

He held steady. "You're very defensive."

She gave a spike of laughter. "Well, you might be, too, if you'd spent a lifetime seeing your face plastered under one hideous headline or another and had to constantly explain yourself to people."

He looked at her for a long, silent moment before speaking. "Perhaps. But I would also realize there were times when it was necessary to explain myself. You're forgetting that we both have the same goal here."

"I don't think so." She stood up. "I think you've had a prejudice against me since we began. Seems to me there's no point in continuing."

He set his pen down. "I'm sorry, you've lost me. What exactly are you saying?"

"That I'm going to talk to Tabitha Monroe." She picked up her purse. "I want you removed from my case."

Five

"You want me removed because I'm asking questions and raising points that make you uncomfortable?"

"No, Dr. Cross, I want you removed because you cannot seem to be objective about me."

"That's not true," he said, calm as can be.

"Yes, it is." Melanie's voice was beginning to sound shrill. "You made up your mind about me before you ever met me. You think I'm some spoiled princess who thinks of children as something to be owned rather than loved and nurtured. Well, I don't know what I can do to prove to you that I'm not like that."

"Saying that you're not necessarily prepared for single parenthood is not the same as saying you're incapable of loving and nurturing."

"It seems to me that you've said both of those things."

"That's crazy," he said angrily, standing up and coming around his desk to where she stood.

"Really?" she asked, looking up at him. "Is that your professional opinion, Doctor? If so, I don't appreciate it at all. Now, if you'll excuse me, I think I'd better leave before I say something I'll regret.''

Melanie didn't wait to hear his response. She ran from his office, and didn't stop till she was at the elevator. Her heart was pounding wildly and she could barely catch her breath.

She couldn't believe she'd had to defend herself against tabloid headlines yet again. And to a psychiatrist, no less! Surely he, of all people, should have been able to see what kind of person she was.

Sometimes she felt that no one would ever see who she really was. People tended to either view her with envy for her means, or with scorn for the supposed scandals she'd caused. Of the two, she usually preferred the latter because at least they didn't pretend to be her friends in order to get money from her.

But Dr. Cross's scorn was something else. It was positively crushing.

She collected herself and hit the elevator button. It opened almost immediately and she stepped in and took a deep breath. With a shaking hand, she pushed the button for the lobby, but a sign for the new maternity wing caught her eye. She pressed the second floor button instead.

The doors opened and Melanie crossed through to the new wing and into a whole new world. While the older part of the hospital was sterile and white, the new wing was alive with primary colors. Waiting rooms had large soft chairs and sofas with several telephones for announcing happy news to waiting family members and friends.

Melanie's chest tightened with every step she took. She wanted a baby so much. She wanted to come stay in this beautiful maternity wing, with all the happy new parents and squeaky new babies. She wanted it so much it hurt. Her eyes burned with unshed tears and she had to press her lips together to keep them from trembling.

A nurses' desk loomed ahead in front of wide swinging doors under a sign that read Nursery. Melanie approached it with hope.

"May I help you?" asked a nurse with short black hair and sharp, elfin features.

"I'd like to go see the babies," Melanie said, smiling even though she knew her weepy eyes betrayed her.

The nurse frowned. "Are you a family member?"

"No, no, I don't know anyone here. I'd just like to look at the babies. You know, through the glass."

"I'm sorry, for security purposes we can't let anyone in."

Melanie realized that she likely looked a little suspicious with her red and probably glassy eyes. "I do work here," she tried. "Over in the staff day-care center."

"You do?" The nurse's tone was doubtful. "And what's your name?"

"Melanie Tourbier."

The nurse began to look at her photocopied staff

list, then stopped and looked up, her features hardening. "Melanie Tourbier, huh? The famous Melanie Tourbier?"

"Well—"

"Look, miss, I don't know what you're up to, but I think you'd better leave before I have to call security."

Melanie's mouth dropped open. "But I *am* Melanie Tourbier!"

The nurse's hand hovered over the security button when a voice behind Melanie drew their attention.

"It's all right, Connie. Let her in."

The voice sent shivers of pleasure down Melanie's spine, even while her brain told her she was still angry. She turned to see Jared Cross directly behind her, as imposing as ever.

"Yes, Dr. Cross." The nurse's face relaxed and she looked at Melanie. "I'm terribly sorry, Miss Tourbier, I didn't know…"

Melanie smiled, hoping to reassure the woman. "Please don't worry about it. I had no business coming here and asking to see the babies like that. I must have sounded nutty. Surely I understand how important security is." She flashed a cold look at Dr. Cross and added, "I'll be leaving now."

"Come on," he said, clearly aware that they had an audience. "Let's talk for a minute."

"I think we've talked enough."

He took her arm and led her through the doors with

a nod to the nurse. "Now that you're here, you might as well go in and take a look."

"Why?" She shook his hand off her arm as soon as they were alone. "So I can see what I'm missing and feel even worse? Do you just want to rub it in, or is this another test?"

"I don't play games."

"You could have fooled me."

"What does that mean?"

"It means I think you do play games. Who dared me to work in the day-care center?"

"Maybe 'dare' was an unfortunate choice of words," he acknowledged. "I only wanted you to see what it was like to take care of children."

"I did. And I love it. So if you were trying to dissuade me, you failed. Sorry to disappoint you."

He gave a light laugh. "I'm not disappointed that you enjoy working with children. Quite the contrary."

"Right."

He looked into her eyes, causing a strange shiver to cross over her. "I get the feeling there's nothing in the world I could say to make you believe me. Even if I told you the sky was blue."

"At this point," Melanie conceded with a wan smile, "I would have to check for myself."

His smile was quick and sincere. "Touché." He drew her forward again. "Now come on, let's look at the babies."

Melanie hesitated. All she'd wanted to do was look

in at the nursery from behind the protective glass, as she'd seen people do on TV. It hadn't occurred to her that there would be a security issue and that it would become an embarrassing scene. If she were to walk out now, though, she'd feel even more foolish.

Yet, at the same time, she didn't quite feel up to sharing the experience with the very man who was trying to stop her from having a baby.

"You know, I think I'll just go on home," she said. "I have an early day tomorrow."

His green eyes held her gaze. "Let's look at the infants. I think it would be good for you."

She could have argued all afternoon, but she was very aware that the nurse who had stopped her was only a few yards away and could probably still hear them. Already she'd probably drawn the conclusion that Melanie was undergoing psychiatric counseling from Dr. Cross. Melanie didn't want to compound that by huffing out. She could only hope the nurse would be as diligent about confidentiality as she was about security.

"I'll show you the way," Jared said, leading Melanie down the wide hallway.

The doors swung open before them and they crossed into another section of the maternity ward. The walls were papered with ducks, dogs and cats and brightly colored letters and numbers. A quick peek inside one or two open doors showed rooms with floral wallpaper, curtains and large rocking chairs.

"This is really lovely," Melanie commented, forgetting, for the moment, her anger with Jared.

"We had some very generous donations," he said pointedly.

Melanie felt her face grow hot. She had donated a large amount to the new maternity wing herself, after deciding to come to the clinic for her fertility treatments, but hadn't wanted to make a big deal of her contribution. "Well, they did a good job with it," she said noncommittally.

"They sure did. With the state-of-the-art equipment they put in, this new wing is a real draw. Not surprisingly, people are coming from all over to use the facility."

"Even as far as England," Melanie commented.

To her surprise, he smiled. "I've heard that." He guided her around the corner where a wide window offered a view of about twenty clear plastic bassinets, each containing a tiny, squirming baby.

Melanie's breath caught in her chest. "Oh, look at them! They're so tiny and helpless."

"Yes, they are."

Believing he was trying to make a point, she flashed him a look, but he was staring at the babies with a peculiar look in his eye. If she didn't know better, and she thought she did, Melanie would have sworn it was a look of longing.

But that was silly. Jared Cross wasn't the sort to long for anything. Especially another human being.

"You don't have a patient on this floor, do you?" Melanie asked.

"No, why?"

"I was just wondering how you happened to come in while I was at the desk."

"I was looking for you."

She was shocked. "You were? How on earth did you know where to find me?"

"Actually, it was just a last-minute hunch. At first I figured you'd huffed on out to your car but when I got on the elevator and was about to push the lobby button, I noticed the sign for the maternity floor and just took a chance that you'd come here."

It was exactly what she'd done herself. Melanie tried to mask her surprise. "Good guess. Why were you looking for me?"

He let out a breath. "If you recall, you didn't leave under the warmest terms."

She did recall. "I didn't feel I had any choice. So what did you want to say to me, Dr. Cross?"

"I wanted…" He glanced down, at the floor or his feet or something other than Melanie's face. "To apologize, actually."

She couldn't believe her ears. "To *apologize?* You? To me? Are you joking?"

He raked his hand through his hair and met her eyes with more uncertainty than she'd seen before. "Look, I shouldn't have said those things to you that way."

"Meaning you should have said them in a different way?" Melanie asked cautiously.

"Meaning I should have asked you from the beginning, rather than accepting the photo at face value. Your explanation made sense, and I'm sorry you had to go through that. It wasn't fair."

Melanie was taken aback. "Why, thank you. I appreciate that." Hope surged in her. "Does this mean you're going to approve my application?"

He didn't answer immediately. Instead, he kept his eyes straight ahead and let out a weary sigh. "Melanie," he said at last, "please try to understand what I'm doing. A lot of things go into this decision. It isn't just about whether you're discreet in front of children. It's about whether this is really the right thing for you and for the child you'd have. We need to continue our counseling in order for me to determine that."

"Great," she said. "So things haven't really changed."

He looked at her. "I'm not out to make your life harder or to keep you from getting what you want, Melanie. Obviously, a week ago I'd never even met you. This isn't personal."

"For me, it's *very* personal."

"Of course it is. That's what might keep you from being totally objective about it. People in your position are running on emotion and sometimes they need a little injection of reality."

"Do I strike you as someone who isn't realistic?"

He didn't answer directly. "Believe me, I'd have the same hesitation about anyone."

"I find that hard to believe."

He looked at her patiently. "Think about it. Try to imagine what you would do if you were me. You're given a dossier on a young woman, still well within her childbearing years, who is used to living on her own and jetting all over the world. There are even newspaper stories—"

"Tabloid."

"—and photos," he added pointedly, "which show that this young woman is used to a very... independent lifestyle."

"Independent, but not wild or irresponsible."

He gave a single nod of his head. "Maybe. But you don't know this woman. Yet you're charged with making a determination as to whether you should, in essence, give her a baby to raise alone." His gaze was penetrating. "What would you do, in my place?"

"First of all, I'd ignore the tabloids and try to see what kind of person this woman really was. If she was kind and capable and dedicated, and had the means to care for a child, I'd give the green light."

"How long would it take you to decide that she was kind and capable and dedicated?" Jared asked. "Remember, there's a baby involved. A whole other person's life, beyond babyhood, beyond childhood, past the cute stages and through some decidedly *un-cute* stages. A parent needs to be committed through all of that. If you were I, how long would you take with that decision?''

Put that way, he had a point, Melanie had to admit. "I don't know," she answered honestly. She sighed. "I suppose I'd take as long as I needed to be sure."

He smiled. "Exactly."

His was a very nice smile, she couldn't help noticing. Another person might have characterized it as kind, though she had her own doubts.

"But I would also make an effort to get to know the woman," Melanie went on. "I wouldn't keep her walking on eggshells, if you'll pardon the pun, while I had one short meeting a week with her."

He raised an eyebrow. "What are you saying, Miss Tourbier?"

"I'm saying that if you need to get to know me in order to green-light this thing, then get to know me. You have my full cooperation. You want me to take IQ tests, Rorschach inkblots, heck, if you want me to salivate like a dog at the sound of the dinner bell, I will. Whatever it takes."

He considered her for a moment, then said, "All right. How about dinner tonight?"

Six

What had he done?

Was he crazy?

Jared couldn't believe his own actions. Asking Melanie Tourbier out to dinner was about as far from professional as he could stray. As soon as the words were out of his mouth, he regretted them, but what could he do? Tell her he was joking? Tell her something had suddenly come up?

Even if he did, he'd just have to figure out another way to meet with her. If not dinner, then lunch or breakfast, because his days were so filled with appointments already.

He was man enough to admit Melanie was right. He had to get to know her. She was here in Mission Creek from London, thousands of miles from home. It wasn't fair for Jared to delay the process any more than was absolutely necessary. As it was, the counseling stage usually took six to eight weeks, and sometimes more. But with a little juggling, he'd probably be able to keep hers closer to the six-week mark. Maybe even five. Whatever his decision, she deserved to have it rendered quickly so that she could move on.

After their initial meeting, Jared had taken a close look at her medical chart and saw that she would, indeed, have a difficult time conceiving, if at all. What was the harm in letting her try? But as long as there was a chance, it was Jared's job to ensure that the child would be coming into a safe, secure environment.

So this dinner he was having with Melanie was professional. Only professional. It might be a little unconventional, but nothing about Melanie's case was what you'd characterize as normal, so his treatment of it needed to be flexible.

That was the thought he held on to as he showered and readied himself to go that evening. Getting to know a patient over a meal was a perfectly valid way to do his job. He had nothing to feel peculiar about. It was work. Business.

That was all there was to it.

It had nothing to do with her long, gleaming dark hair or the light in her sky-blue eyes. Sure, he'd noticed the way they lit up when she smiled and how they danced when she talked about something she cared about, but they didn't influence his opinion of her. Neither did her smooth, pale skin or the mesmerizing curve of her mouth. Other men might be swayed by that kind of thing, but not Jared, he thought as he reached down and turned the shower dial to make the water a little cooler.

Jared couldn't allow himself to be swayed by a pretty face or a knockout figure. It hadn't always been easy, that was for sure. When he'd first seen Melanie on the elevator, he'd had a small stirring of interest for the first time in just about as long as he could remember. When she'd come into his office as a patient, he had met her with a sense of disbelief that turned to inevitability. Of course she would end up being his patient. That was just the way his luck with women went. He should have guessed it when she'd pressed the eighth-floor button.

It was a little disappointing at first, although he hadn't exactly banked on the idea of ever seeing her again. But he thought he'd slipped into his professional role as counselor fairly easily. Obviously she disagreed with his methods, but he would have been the same with any single young woman who came to him under the same circumstances.

Wouldn't he?

He thought long and hard about the answer. There had been Selma Indio a few years back. She'd lost her husband in an accident and wanted to have a sibling for their then two-year-old son. Jared had had no trouble whatsoever being objective about her case. He'd seen her for about a month and a half, listening to her concerns, her reasons and the practical details that made her a good candidate, like the fact that she was surrounded by her very close-knit family.

Jared had sponsored her candidacy and she'd gone on to have a beautiful, healthy baby girl and Jared had no regrets. That was six years ago and in that time he'd had no cause to rethink his decision.

Melanie, however, was a different case. She was a single woman who'd lost her family at an early age and had gone on to live a lively single life. His concerns were legitimate. He wasn't going to back down. But maybe his approach had been a little too impersonal. Maybe he really needed to look at the *woman* more than just the *case*. After all, Melanie Tourbier was clearly a very special person. Her desire for a family was sincere and touching. Maybe Jared could still help her.

Somehow.

But why was he so hesitant to do so? He guessed it was because it was hard to reconcile the wild, irresponsible woman he'd read about in the press with the tender, almost shy woman he was getting to know now.

Which was exactly why he needed to take this extra time to get to know her.

Half an hour later, he was in his car driving to the address Melanie had given him for her temporary home at The Aldon Towers, a huge luxury apartment building on the west side of town.

He parked out front and went through the revolving door into a gleaming lobby, where he was stopped by an imposing security desk.

"May I help you, sir?" the guard asked.

"Miss Tourbier, please."

The guard's eyes lit up. "Ah, Miss Tourbier. One moment, please."

"It's all right, Wendell," Melanie said, rounding

the corner just as he lifted the telephone receiver. "Thank you."

"You're very welcome, Miss Tourbier," Wendell answered with what sounded to Jared like reverence.

And Jared could see why. Melanie, dressed in a simple dark-blue silk dress that looked like something from Grace Kelly's closet, looked stunning. If she wore makeup, it was only enough to enhance her naturally pretty features: pink lips, bright eyes, slightly flushed cheeks. Her dark hair fell around her shoulders in glossy waves that made Jared's hands ache to touch her.

It was a disturbingly *unprofessional* impulse.

"Ready?" he asked, shoving his hands into his pockets.

She smiled the kind of smile that Jared was certain made Wendell's heart skip a beat.

"I'm absolutely ready."

Jared cleared his throat. Suddenly his collar felt hot and tight. "Let's go." He gestured toward the door then followed her out into the sultry evening air. "My car is right here." He pointed at the refurbished 1965 Ford Mustang.

"Look at that!" Melanie gasped. "Where did you get it?"

"Ace Carson over at Lone Star Autos found it for me. They don't usually deal with old domestics like this, but he did it as a favor."

"I love it." She ran her hand across the hood of the car. "My father had one of these in candy-apple red. It was his pride and joy. Well, besides Mother and me, that is. He loved that car.''

''What happened to it?'' Jared said, opening the car door for her.

''I don't know. I suppose that's one of the things his lawyer sold after he died.''

''I'm sorry,'' Jared said, mentally kicking himself. He'd been trying so hard to make light conversation that somehow he'd forgotten for the moment that her parents had both died some time back. He shut the door behind her and went around to his side.

''It's all right,'' she said to him when he got in. ''I actually like to talk about my parents. The subject doesn't come up very often anymore.''

''Do you remember them well?'' he asked as he turned the ignition key. The car rumbled to life, throbbing beneath them.

She leaned back in her seat and looked out the window to her right. ''Sometimes I feel like I barely remember them at all,'' she said with a sigh. ''Then other times I think I remember too much. And if I couldn't remember, then I wouldn't know what I was missing. I guess that sounds kind of silly.''

''It doesn't sound silly at all,'' Jared said, pulling the car into traffic on Aldon Boulevard. ''I know just how you feel.''

''Really?'' She turned to face him. He could feel her gaze on his profile. ''Did you lose your parents when you were young, too?''

''Yes.'' He didn't offer more. He couldn't.

"I'm sorry to hear that." She must have picked up on his tension because she didn't ask him to elaborate. Instead she asked, "So where are we going?"

"I've made reservations at the Empire Room over at the Lone Star Country Club. I hope that's all right with you. They serve everything from steak to pasta." It was a place that Jared often went when he was conducting business. He wanted this evening to feel like business, not a date.

"That sounds wonderful," she said, sounding genuinely enthusiastic.

He could see, even in the dim interior lighting, that her eyes danced. She was very, very pretty. Even more than he'd realized before.

"I've never been to the club," she was saying, "but I've heard so much about it."

"You can't come to Mission Creek without hearing about it," Jared said, readjusting his grip on the wheel. This isn't a date, he reminded himself again, although he shouldn't have needed to. It had been a long time since he'd been on a date. Maybe that was why he was struggling. He was so out of practice that even this business meeting felt intimate. "I thought it was a good choice for this evening because it's quiet so we can talk. We have a lot to accomplish in a little time."

She gave him a look. "If you're trying to remind me that this is all business, you needn't. I'm very aware of why I'm here."

She was on to him.

"Good," he said, his voice more clipped than he'd intended. "We understand each other."

"If that were true we wouldn't be here," Melanie mused. "But we do at least agree on this one thing."

Jared had the curious feeling that he was at a disadvantage whenever he was talking to Melanie. He felt she had him completely figured out, while he was still scraping away at her surface.

He turned the car into the long driveway of the Lone Star Country Club and, after a couple of minutes of thick silence, parked out front.

He stopped the car and got out. By the time he got to Melanie's door, she'd already let herself out.

Good. This was not a date. It shouldn't feel like one.

"What a nice place!" Melanie said. "You really get a sense of space out here."

With hundreds of flat, manicured acres surrounding the club, that was certainly true. "It's a far cry from London, I guess."

"Oh, yes, a very far cry," she agreed. "I'd forgotten what it was like to have so much breathing room. It's nice." She looked over the property in the distance. "Very nice. It reminds me of our place in Dallas."

"That's right, I'd forgotten you have some Texan in you."

She smiled. "Enough to feel like I'm coming home."

"Really?" Jared was surprised. "Does that mean you're thinking of staying here?"

She took a long breath and let it out. "No, I don't think so. My home is in London now. This is just like a wonderful vacation. Like traveling back in time to an era that was simpler and happier."

"But not real?"

She looked off in the distance. "Not anymore."

They walked up the steps to the front door of the club and Jared opened it for Melanie. When they got inside, the maître d' gave a broad smile. "Good evening, Dr. Cross."

"Marcus." Jared nodded.

"And this must be the lovely Miss Tourbier," Marcus went on, extending his arms in a broad, welcoming gesture. "Dr. Cross told me you would be joining him this evening. I met your mother and father many years ago when I worked at the Golden Palace in Dallas. You are every bit as lovely as your mother."

Melanie's cheeks turned a becoming pink and she smiled graciously. "Thank you. You're very kind."

"Not at all. Your table is right this way." Marcus led them through the doorway into the opulent dining room.

Jared wondered if the gilded interior seemed as over-the-top to Melanie as it did to him, or if she was accustomed to gilded chairs, fine china and chandeliers hovering over every table. Perhaps she was even tired of this kind of glitz. Maybe he should have taken her over to the Saddlebag instead, a down-home country bar with a jukebox and peanuts on the floor, just to show her something different.

But he didn't need to show her something different, he reminded himself. He wasn't out to impress her or show her a good time.

This was business.

"Is Pedro in the kitchen tonight?" Jared asked as Marcus stopped at a private table in the corner and pulled a chair out for Melanie.

Marcus shook his head. "He's on a much-needed vacation. This week we have a visiting chef from Chez Martinique in Nice."

Melanie clapped her hands together. "Not Jean-Pierre Lumier!"

Marcus looked surprised. "Why, yes, it is."

"Oh, he's marvelous! What good luck to come here on a night when he's visiting." She beamed at Jared. "You made a very good choice."

Her smile made his chest feel tight. "I'd like to take credit for it, but I had no idea." In fact, he still had no idea whom they were talking about. Although he had the means to travel the world now, his lifestyle hadn't changed very much. Truth was, he was much more comfortable at the Saddlebag himself than here in the Empire Room.

"Enjoy your meal," Marcus said, and left them.

When he had gone, Melanie said, "I can't get over how friendly people are here."

"You seem to bring it out in them."

She lowered her chin and looked up at him through

dark-fringed lashes. "I don't seem to bring it out in you, though, do I?"

She brought more out in him than she realized. More than he'd realized before tonight. "Does it matter?" he asked, his voice gruff.

"I suppose not." She shrugged and picked up the menu. "This is, after all, just business."

"Yes," he agreed, without much conviction.

She looked at him over her menu, her blue eyes sparkling as if she were amused by him.

Or maybe it was just a trick of the flickering candlelight.

"You look like the cat who swallowed the canary," Jared said. "What's going on?"

She shrugged. "I just have a good feeling about things. I'm glad you asked for this dinner because I think it means you're opening your mind to me and my situation a little."

He raised an eyebrow. "I've always been open-minded to you and your situation."

She laughed outright. "I don't think so, Dr. Cross. But I guess I shouldn't blame you entirely. A lot of people who don't know me have the wrong impression about me."

"What's the right impression?" he asked. "If you were going to describe yourself to someone else, what would you say?"

"That I'm not the kind of person who likes to synopsize myself into a list of tidy little adjectives."

The waiter interrupted and asked for their orders.

Melanie and Jared each ordered the filet of beef with Swiss chard and garlic potatoes. Without thinking, Jared also ordered a vintage red wine from the Tourbier-Solange vineyard. It wasn't until he'd handed the menus back to the waiter and they were alone that he realized Melanie was looking at him oddly.

"What's the matter?" he asked.

"Nothing. It's just…" She smiled. "That wine you just ordered was my father's own reserve. It was his favorite. He and my mother always drank it on special occasions and holidays."

Tourbier-Solange. Incredibly, Jared hadn't even made the connection with Melanie. He hoped it wasn't a sore spot with her. "How long has it been since you lost your parents?" he asked.

"Fifteen years." She looked down, but not before he saw the sorrow come into her eyes. "Half my life."

"Fifteen is awfully young to lose your parents. It must have been very difficult."

She looked into his eyes. "It was. For a long, long time. I'm all right now, of course." She smiled sadly. "Although there are times when I'm keenly aware of what I'm missing."

"Like when?"

"Well, the obvious times, like Christmas and Thanksgiving and birthdays and so on." She paused while the waiter reappeared and poured the wine. "But there are a million other times when I miss them. Like when my car breaks down and I want my dad to come fix it, or when I'm having a party and I want my mother's recipe for cheese puffs.''

"Surely you have people to help with all of that. A mechanic, a cook…?''

She smiled. "Yes, of course. But the thing is, when I was growing up, we didn't live extravagantly.''

"No?'' Jared asked, interested.

"No, not really. Granted, there were vacations and good schools and so on, but when the kitchen sink clogged, the first person my mother would call was my father. And he could usually fix it.'' She laughed. "And if he couldn't, he'd dicker with the local plumber over the price.''

Jared liked the man already, even though he'd never get the chance to know him. "Your lifestyle is different now, I gather.''

She nodded. "The suburban cul-de-sac with families and kids didn't seem like the right place for me anymore.''

"Why not?''

She looked at him as if to say *Be serious.* "I don't think I'd fit in. At least not without becoming some pitiful figure that the neighbors talked about in private.'' She shrugged. "It's not the place for me right now.''

"What if you weren't alone? What if all the choices were open to you? What would you like?''

"If I could choose *any* life for myself?''

He nodded.

Her eyes grew faraway and she considered for a

long moment before answering. "I'd like that house in the suburbs. I'd like neighbors to barbecue with on Sundays, and kids shrieking and playing in the sun during the day instead of weekends on some yacht in the Mediterranean. I'd like brightly colored plastic toys littering the yards around me instead of fussy little gardens and iron gates. I'd like to spend Friday nights making popcorn and watching *Mary Poppins* instead of attending premières and political fundraisers or crowded parties." She gave a quick, embarrassed smile. "You probably don't believe that, but it's true."

Jared swallowed but his throat felt tight. The life she had described was the one he'd always hoped for as a child in the orphanage, the one he'd spent a lifetime expecting—somewhere in the deepest corners of his mind. It was a vision he could never quite shake. "I believe you," he said softly.

Hope lit her eyes. "You do?"

He nodded. "It's the American dream, isn't it? House, dogs, kids. Who doesn't want that?"

"I know plenty of people who don't want it. In fact, it's a lifestyle they avoid like the plague."

"Friends of yours?"

"Some."

"So you share their partying lifestyle instead."

"It would seem that way. Especially to someone on the outside."

"So tell me, why do you do the yacht cruises and fancy parties if you don't enjoy them?"

"What else am I going to do?" she asked. "That's what's expected of me. If I refuse those invitations, it will just make my friends worry about me and try even harder to get me to go out."

"But aren't there things you'd enjoy doing?"

She sighed. "I can't date and go to dinner and a movie the way other single girls can any more than I can buy that dream house and live the family life by myself. I'm not able to move around normally because people know who I am and tend to approach me." She glanced around and lowered her voice. "Not here in Mission Creek so much, but you'd be surprised how often I'm recognized when I go out."

Actually, he wouldn't. The hospital had been buzzing with news of her presence in town ever since she'd arrived and had her first visit in his office. The staff was respectful of her privacy, but amongst themselves their enthusiasm at having a celebrity in their midst couldn't be contained.

"How would that change if you had a baby?" he asked, reminding himself that he had an objective to work toward and he had to stop looking at her eyes and start looking at her circumstances instead.

"It would change completely," she started, but was interrupted by the arrival of their food.

Although Jared was irritated at the interruption, for reasons he didn't want to examine, Melanie was very gracious to the starstruck wait staff, thanking them profusely for their prompt service and attention.

When they were finally alone again, he urged her

to continue. "You were saying how things would be different if you had a child."

"Boy, you don't miss a beat, do you?" She cut a small piece of beef and popped it into her mouth. "Wow, this is terrific. They ought to try and persuade Jean-Pierre to stay."

"International types don't usually stay in Mission Creek," he said dryly, taking a bite of the steak. It was good, he had to admit.

"I don't know why not," she said, lifting her water glass. "It's a charming town."

"I agree, but I think it's a bit dull for most jet-setters. No gambling, no high seas. No state dinners."

"In other words, heaven." She gave a light laugh and said, "Back to your question, which I promise I'm not avoiding, of how my life will change when I have a child. For one thing, I'll be able to stay in and live the quiet life I want without people suspecting there's something wrong with me."

"Something wrong?"

"Yes." She tapped her temple. "You know, depression or anxiety or something. Every time I decline an invitation in order to stay home and watch TV or something, it's met with a thousand questions about why I'm not up to going out or if I'm sure I should stay home alone. My friends are well-meaning but overprotective."

He could see her point. "So if you had a child you'd have, in essence, the perfect excuse."

She nodded. "Not that I want to have a child

merely to get out of social engagements.'' She gave him a look. "So don't ask me that next.''

He smiled. "It never even crossed my mind.''

"Nonsense. Everything crosses your mind, I can see it.'' She leaned toward him and looked deep into his eyes, which put her disconcertingly close. "You're always thinking and calculating things, aren't you? If I'd ordered a vegetable entrée, you would have wondered if I was a vegetarian and, if so, would I give my child a healthy, balanced diet.''

Jared laughed and lifted his wineglass. "I hope I don't seem *that* micro-managerial.''

"You're just doing your job, I understand. And, for the record, I'm *not* a vegetarian but even if I were, I would see to it that my baby got all the necessary nutrients.''

"I believe you.'' He sipped the wine. It was truly superb, dry with just a hint of something sweet. Melanie's father had good taste. He set the glass down and noticed that Melanie hadn't touched hers. "You're not drinking the wine.''

An expression he couldn't read flashed in her eyes before she looked down. "No, I think I shouldn't right now.''

"Why not?''

She met his eyes, almost apologetically. "I don't want to have any alcohol while I'm hoping to get pregnant.''

"Ah. I see.'' They were never going to stray very

far from that point. "So, tell me, do you have other close family? Brothers, sisters, aunts, uncles?"

She shook her head and took another sip of her water. "No, it's just me." She glanced at him. "For now, at least. I am, of course, hoping that will change soon."

In that moment, Jared wanted to do whatever he could to help her. She was such a sweet soul, so gentle and well-intentioned. Had her parents lived, he imagined they would have been a very close family. Maybe then she wouldn't have been in such a hurry for her own baby.

That was a problem, as far as Jared was concerned. Loneliness wasn't a good reason for having a child. If only she would open herself up to the possibility of a relationship with someone. It would make everything fall into place, Jared was sure of it.

"What about you?" she asked.

He hesitated then gave the smallest smile. "Aren't I the one who's supposed to be asking the questions?"

She made a broad gesture. "Go right ahead."

He wanted to question her professionally, to do his job, make a learned assessment and send her on her way, wherever that might be. He knew that his interest in her continued to border on something other than professional and that the best thing he could do—both for himself and for her—was finish the job he had to do and then get away from her.

"How long have you wanted to be a mother?"

She took a deep breath. "Well, I've always wanted to be a mother. Even when I was a child, I can remember putting my Baby Tender Love into a bathtub full of bubble bath and then putting her in diapers and baby clothes." She closed her eyes for a moment and smiled. "I still remember the smell of those clean new diapers."

"This was before you lost your parents, obviously." So her desire for starting a family didn't come from losing one.

She nodded. "Oh, yes. I guess my mother made being a mom look so fun that I wanted to be just like her." She gave a wistful smile. "I still do. She was a wonderful woman. She lived a happy life."

He watched her, wishing he could take the pain from her eyes. Melanie Tourbier was a good person, that much was clear. Her intentions were good. Her heart was in the right place.

That alone didn't make her a good candidate for fertility treatments and single parenthood, of course, but it at least shed some light on her desire. It helped Jared to see it, and approach it, in a different way.

"When did you start seriously thinking of having a baby?" he asked. "Of taking this next step?"

She took a sip of water and set the glass down. "When I was married a few years ago."

"You tried to start a family then?"

"Oh, yes. We tried very hard to get pregnant. That's when I found out about…my problem conceiving."

"I see." He recalled the name of the specialist on her chart. The doctor was internationally renowned. "Did you try artificial insemination then?"

"No, just fertility drugs. I guess it wasn't enough. The marriage ended without children, obviously, but my determination to have them didn't go away, even though my husband did."

"Why have you focused on having children alone rather than trying to find another man?"

"Who says I haven't tried to find another man?"

He'd just assumed she hadn't. "Have you?"

"I've dated, of course. But for the most part I've been on my own for the past few years and have come to realize more and more that the likelihood of my finding a really good man is very slim."

"You don't think there's even one man out there who might suit you?" Jared asked incredulously.

She shook her head. "Don't get me wrong. It's not that I'm overly picky or anything. It's just that my experience with men hasn't been all that great. I've given my trust away to the wrong people so often that I think I'm just about tapped out."

"And you've given up on love, so to speak."

"Yes," she said, looking at him evenly. "I have. But I have not given up on having a family."

Jared was surprised at this revelation. It was the first time Melanie had mentioned her real reasons for not having a relationship with a man. This desire to have a baby on her own wasn't rebellion or selfishness or boredom or anything else. It was coming from a feeling that she'd never find a man she could trust, so she was going to move on and do the rest of the family alone.

She was just misguided.

"So if you believed it was possible to find a good man, you wouldn't be here?" he asked, the germ of an idea formulating.

She thought before answering. "I probably would still be here," she said. "I just might not be here alone."

"So let me get this straight. If, theoretically, the perfect man for you came along, you'd be willing to put this artificial insemination idea on hold. Even temporarily."

She gave him a patient look. "I've already explored possibilities in that area."

"Okay, but theoretically," he persisted. "What if the right guy came along tomorrow?"

"I'd drop dead of shock."

"Melanie, I'm serious."

"Okay, theoretically I would, obviously. That's why I'd put this plan on hold for the past five years. But guess what? He didn't show. I guess he doesn't exist. So I'm moving on without him."

"Unless he shows up."

"Which he's not going to do. Especially not tonight, which is about when he'd need to get here in order to stop me from moving forward."

Jared didn't argue. Clearly there was no point. Melanie Tourbier wasn't one to be swayed by words. She needed action. She needed things to be tangible. He could appreciate that. He certainly understood it.

He was the same way.

Now, it was as if a door had opened. Jared knew exactly what he had to do, for his own purposes and for Melanie's. The answer was as clear and simple as could be.

He had to find Melanie Tourbier a husband.

Seven

Melanie felt her dinner meeting with Dr. Cross had gone very well, so the next day when he asked her to drop by his office before lunch, she hoped it was because he wanted to tell her he'd approved her for fertility treatments.

Her heart hammered in her chest as she headed for his office. This might be it. Maybe her dream was finally going to come true. She couldn't wait.

When she got to his office, the secretary was nowhere to be seen and the waiting room was empty. Melanie went to his door and was about to knock when she heard two men's voices and a spike of laughter from inside.

Frowning, she knocked quietly. "Dr. Cross?"

The door opened and Jared was standing there, smiling as she hadn't seen him do since he'd come to the day care to see the children. "Melanie!" he said, his voice unusually gregarious. "Thanks for coming." He stepped aside and gestured toward his desk. "Please have a seat."

Melanie entered, giving Jared a puzzled look. What had happened to make him so friendly to her all of a sudden?

Then she saw the other man. He was tall and slim, very tan, with short brown hair and wide, dark eyes. He was wearing tennis shorts and a pale-yellow knit shirt, and had a white sweater knotted around his neck.

"Melanie, this is Lance Freedman," Jared said, smiling from her to the man and back again. "He's the tennis pro over at the country club."

"Nice to meet you," she said, smiling but still wondering what this was all about.

"Oh, honey, it's *so* nice to meet you," Lance returned, opening his arms flamboyantly. "Come here and give me a hug."

Jared smiled and nodded his encouragement at her.

Unable to think of a graceful way out of it, Melanie stepped forward and hugged the man gingerly before looking back at Jared. "I'm sorry, did I misunderstand? I thought you wanted to have a meeting with me, but am I interrupting here?"

"No, no," Jared said. "Lance and I were just talking sports."

She still didn't get it. "You were."

"My friend Perry has qualified for the Olympics," Lance explained. "We're very excited."

Although none of this cleared up her confusion, Melanie knew a polite interest was called for. "Really?" she asked. "In what event?"

"Synchronized swimming."

"Ah." She searched for some appropriate response. "That *is* very exciting. But, still, I seem to be interrupting a private conversation...."

Jared cleared his throat. "Lance is quite an athlete himself. He ranked third in the U.S. Open a couple of years ago."

"That scamp Andre Agassi swept the men's singles," Lance said with a practiced smile. "I'd hate him if he weren't such a super guy."

"Do you play tennis, Melanie?" Jared asked, sitting down in his chair and leaning into it as if they were all kicking back with a beer.

She looked at him, puzzled, for a moment, then answered, "Um, yes, I've played some. I'm afraid I'm not very good, but—"

"Well, why not let Lance help you with that? He's the best. Lance, are you taking on new pupils?"

"All the time."

Melanie felt as if she'd walked into an episode of *The Twilight Zone*. The man in front of her *looked* like Jared Cross, but he wasn't acting like him. When did he get so chipper? When did he talk, or even think, about anything other than his work?

"I'll keep it in mind," she said. "In the meantime, what was it you wanted to see me about, Dr. Cross?"

"I'd better tootle along and let you two chat by yourselves," Lance said. "I have a lesson at five-thirty, then Perry and I are going out for a celebratory dinner at the Empire Room."

Jared looked disappointed. "Do you really have to go already?"

"Time is money, honey." Lance flashed a brilliant smile. "Melanie, it was a delight to meet you. Especially since I've heard so much about you."

"You have?" she asked, looking suspiciously at Jared.

"Yes, indeedy," Lance said, then noticed her look. "Oh, not from the doc. What I should have said is that I've *read* a lot about you. I've been a fan of yours for a very long time."

"I see," she said, knowing just the kind of thing he must have read. "Thank you, but I haven't really done anything fan-worthy."

"Nonsense. That layout in *House and Home* showed some of the most innovative, thrilling decorating I've ever seen. I'd just love to meet your interior decorator."

He probably would, Melanie thought privately. Lance was just the kind of guy Georg loved.

"Plus Jared was just telling me what a great gal you are," Lance went on, winking at Jared. "I don't think I'm the only rabid Melanie Tourbier fan around here."

Melanie couldn't keep the look of complete puzzlement off her face.

Jared cleared his throat. "Lance, do you have a card or something so Melanie can get ahold of you? About those tennis lessons, I mean."

"I surely do." Lance took a tennis-ball-shaped business card out of his back pocket and handed it to Melanie.

His name was written in wedding-invitation script across the top of the ball and underneath it read *Tennis Instruction and Outfitting,* whatever that meant. Beneath that, looking out of place, was the more masculine logo of the Lone Star Country Club.

"Thanks," Melanie said. "I'm not sure when or if I'll get around to taking tennis lessons, but I'll definitely keep you in mind if I do."

"Okeydoke," Lance said cheerfully. "I hope to see you on the clay soon. Jared, fabulous to see you. Thanks so much for the tickets."

Was it her imagination, or did Jared's face go slightly red?

"Sure, Lance. Anytime."

"Tickets?" Melanie asked, wondering why Jared was looking at her so self-consciously.

"Somehow Jared scored tickets for a sold-out concert next Friday night," Lance explained to Melanie. "You're sure you don't want to come?" he asked Jared.

Now Jared's face was definitely red. "Er, no. But what about you, Melanie?"

This was weird.

If she didn't know better, she'd swear he was trying to set her up with Lance. Of course, that was obviously out of the question, so what *was* going on with Jared Cross? Had someone spiked his coffee? Was he having a strange reaction to some sort of new medication?

"Actually, that's okay," she said. "I'm sure you'll have a great time, Lance. Enjoy."

"I will indeed," Lance said, making a grand sweep for the door. "Take care, you two."

Melanie smiled. "Ta-ta."

"Later, Lance," Jared said, looking somewhat resigned.

When Lance was gone, Melanie turned back to Jared. "What was it you wanted to see me about, Jared? Surely it wasn't about tennis lessons with Lance."

"What? No, of course not. Lance just happened to stop by when you were coming up and it occurred to me that the two of you might have some things in common."

"Like what?"

He shrugged. "Tennis, for one thing."

"Hmm." Something told her he wasn't giving her the whole truth, but no other plausible explanation came to her. "Well, with my work at the day care and the procedure I hope to begin *soon*—" she gave him a pointed look "—I don't really think I'll have much time for tennis lessons. But thanks for thinking of me. Anyway, why did you want me to come up?"

"Just some administrative stuff," he said vaguely. "Insurance. My secretary didn't make a copy of your insurance card when you first came in and the administrator called me about it."

"Actually your secretary *did* copy the card," Melanie said. "In fact, I saw her do it and then put it into my file folder."

Jared picked up a folder that was marked Tourbier, Melanie J. and opened it. "So she did," he said, leafing through the papers. "Sorry about that. I don't know what the administrators were thinking, but I'll make sure they get this."

"Was that all?" Melanie asked, disappointed he wasn't following up with encouraging news about her status.

"That's it."

She stood up. "Okay, I guess I'll see you on Friday for our scheduled appointment."

He nodded. "Unless something comes up before then."

"Like what?"

"I don't know, anything." He shrugged. "The paperwork never seems to end around here. But hopefully they have everything they need from you now."

"I can't imagine they don't." Melanie started for the door. "I'll see you in a few days."

"Three," he said.

She stopped and looked back at him. Something about the way he looked at her gave her pause. There was warmth in his eyes. And they were very nice eyes, too. "Three, then." She smiled.

He smiled back. Then, seeming to catch himself, he looked to the papers on his desk and began to shuffle them. "Have a nice day."

"You, too," she said, and left, wondering what on earth had just happened.

* * *

Well, *that* hadn't gone well, Jared thought when Melanie had gone.

What was wrong with her?

Here he'd introduced her to a nice man, a good-looking guy who was healthy and young—perfect father material, biologically speaking—and she'd barely even looked at him. Every time Jared had opened the door for the two of them to get together, Melanie had slammed it shut.

Maybe the reason she couldn't find the right man was because she was too damn picky.

On the other hand, perhaps it wasn't entirely her fault.

Maybe she was so jaded about men these days she didn't even see them as prospective partners anymore. She was too guy-shy.

Or maybe Lance hadn't been her type. Certainly he was a good physical specimen, if one was merely looking for biological father material, but Jared wasn't trying to get her a sperm donor, he wanted to get her a husband. So Lance hadn't worked out.

Jared would just try again.

After all, he *wanted* to help Melanie, he truly did. She would make a fine wife and mother, he was sure of that. Her beauty was one thing, a nice bonus to be sure, but she was a sweet, gentle soul on the inside. That was what struck Jared the most. Melanie Tourbier somehow managed to combine physical beauty with intelligence, culture, breeding and a refreshing down-to-earth quality. The man for her had to appreciate all of that.

Jared's thoughts were interrupted by a knock at the door.

"Come in," he called, half expecting, half hoping it was her.

It wasn't.

"Heard you had a loose wire in one of your lights in here," Marvin Doddi, the building superintendent, said. Marvin was a stocky man of southern Italian descent. His dark hair was thinning, but his eyes were bright and sharp. He was a good, honest, hardworking man. Jared had always liked him.

"Sorry to get to you so late, Doc, but I've had lots of calls this morning." Marvin swabbed his brow with his forearm.

"It's no problem, Marvin," Jared said. "It's that light over there." He pointed. "I looked at it myself. The socket's overheating, so I think it just needs to be replaced. I would have done it myself if I could have turned off the power without putting the whole building out."

"Could have saved me some time," Marvin said with a smile. "But the power main is in the basement." He took a two-way radio out of his pocket and called down to have someone shut off one of the circuits while he worked on it.

"So you've had a lot of calls this morning?" Jared asked.

"Yes," Marvin said. "A lot of folks are complaining that their phones aren't working right. Matter of fact, my son Tony just came in from Dallas to visit and said he tried all morning to get through, but no luck. Finally he just came in and had them call me from the front desk."

"How is Tony?" Jared vaguely remembered a dark-haired young man who used to come with Marvin to work sometimes. It was hard to believe he was grown-up already.

"Well, he's just split up with his girl." Marvin scratched his head ruefully. "Kid's standards are too high, I say, but who listens to the old man?"

Jared gave a dry laugh. "Tell me about it. Some people get this idea into their head about what the perfect person is like, and when their significant other doesn't measure up—because they *can't*—they dump them."

"My boy's done it at least five times this year," Marvin agreed. "You know someone like that, too, huh?"

"Yup. I don't know what she wants, but she thinks there's no one out there who's honest enough."

"Honest? That's all she's looking for? Should be a dime a dozen."

"You'd think." Jared tapped his pen on the desk. "There must be something else. She's just meeting the wrong kinds of guys." He stopped tapping and looked at Marvin. "Say, what does Tony do for a living?"

There was just a moment's hesitation before Marvin answered, "He…well, he works in the arts."

"Really." Jared thought of Melanie. If she didn't like athletic types, maybe she'd like the artistic sort. Jared could certainly vouch for Tony's family. "An artist, huh?"

Marvin chuckled. "I guess you'd say that. He's struggling, but who isn't these days?"

"True."

"His mama will cook him some good food, get him fortified and send him back out into the world in a few weeks. He comes home every once in a while for that, though he wouldn't admit it."

"I see. And he's, what, midtwenties?"

"Why are you asking all these questions, Dr. Cross? You working on another study or something?"

"No, nothing like that." Jared smiled conspiratorially. "I'm working on a different kind of project. And I think Tony might be just the man for the job."

Melanie was surprised when Jared came into the day care that afternoon and asked for her.

"More paperwork?" she asked with a sly smile.

"What?" He looked blank. "Oh. No. Actually, I've come to ask a favor of you."

This news surprised her. "A favor? You're kidding."

"Why would you say that?"

"Because you don't strike me as the kind of guy who asks for favors very often."

"As a matter of fact, I don't like to ask, but it's for a friend of mine and he could really use the help."

This sounded serious. "Sure, if I can help, I will," she said, ushering him to a quiet corner of the day care. "What is it?"

"I believe you mentioned once that your family owned several galleries in Europe."

She frowned. "I'm not sure I mentioned that but, yes, we do."

"Well, there's a fellow who works here, great guy, Marvin. He's the building superintendent. You may have met him."

"I don't think so."

"I'll introduce you. He's really a great guy. Honest, upstanding. Anyway, his son works in the arts and Marvin was thinking that maybe you could help give him some advice about, you know—" he splayed his arms "—succeeding as an artist."

"Gosh, I'm not sure how helpful I can be with that kind of thing," Melanie began. "I mean, I appreciate the arts, obviously, and my parents were great supporters of underfed talent, but I'm afraid I don't really know all that much about it myself."

They were interrupted by five-year-old Peter Wickham, with whom Melanie had spent the past half hour coloring.

"Melny, Melny," Peter said, tugging on her pant

leg. "I drew you a picture!" He handed her a smudged piece of newsprint with two stick figures surrounded by red dots.

"What's this?" she asked, bending down to his level.

Peter leaned forward and said, in a stage whisper, "It's you and him." He pointed at Jared.

"It is?" She pointed at the red dots, which she suspected might be chicken pox or something. "What are these?"

"Hearts!" Peter cried, then dissolved into giggles.

Melanie felt her face grow hot. "Honey, Dr. Cross and I aren't... We don't have..." She looked at Jared. "Help me out, here, you're the professional."

He looked equally bemused, but before he could say a word, Peter whipped the picture out of her hand and said, "Ooh! I forgot to add the baby!" and ran off to the crayon center.

Melanie looked at Jared, suddenly feeling self-conscious. "Kids, huh?" She laughed nervously. "You never know what they're thinking."

"It's perfectly normal," Jared explained. "A lot of them think in terms of family. Everything's family, whether it's people or cars or dogs or whatever. Very often kids will draw three of something, make one of them small, and call it the baby. It's a way of defining their own place in the world."

She didn't ask where the hearts came into the picture or why the child would choose Jared and herself as a couple. Whatever his answer would be, she knew he couldn't understand it any better than she could. It must have just been a fluke. A meaningless fancy on the part of Peter. Not a premonition.

Although she liked adding a baby.

Jared cleared his throat, uncharacteristically awkward. "So you were saying about the galleries...?"

She was glad for the change of subject. "Oh, yes. They're all run by other people. I really have no hand in them at all."

"Maybe you could help steer Tony in the direction of those folks, then," Jared suggested.

Melanie shrugged. "I'd be glad to do what I can."

"That's perfect," Jared said, looking as if he'd just solved the last math problem on a final exam. "Marvin will be really glad to hear it. Can I have my secretary set up a meeting between the two of you?"

That sounded harmless enough. "That will be fine. You know my hours here. Something around lunchtime would probably work pretty well. I doubt anything I have to say will take longer than that."

"Don't be modest," Jared said, the expression in his eyes intense. "You have a lot to offer."

For a fraction of a moment Melanie wondered if she was seeing something personal in the depths of Jared's eyes, rather than the professional concern she usually saw. He almost looked eager, although it was hard to say why. Maybe he was just anxious that his friend's son get some help.

That was probably it.

"I'll do my best," she said, trying to reassure him.

"That's great," Jared said. "And I'll see you, when, Friday I think?"

She smiled. "I hope we can come to a conclusion then. Or, rather, I hope you can."

"I hope so, too," he said cryptically.

On Thursday morning, Jared was just taking his bag lunch from the drawer and getting ready to go to the lounge when his door burst open like a shot.

Melanie Tourbier stormed in, her blue eyes blazing. "Just *what* are you trying to do?"

"Excuse me?"

"What are you trying to do?"

"I'm trying to eat lunch. Why?"

His secretary hurried in after Melanie. "Miss Tourbier, please!" She gave a helpless look at Jared. "I told her she couldn't come in unannounced but she did it anyway. It's not my fault."

"It's fine, Wendy," he said.

Wendy didn't move.

"You can go," he said to her. "I'll take care of this."

"No, *I'll* take care of this," Melanie returned angrily.

He sighed and said to the inert Wendy, "We'll take care of this. Go on to lunch."

"I already went to lunch," Wendy said.

Jared gave an exasperated sigh. "Then why don't you make Miss Tourbier a nice hot cup of tea?"

Wendy shrugged. "Okay..."

He knew she wanted some good gossip, but he wasn't going to open himself up to it. "Go, Wendy," he commanded.

Reluctantly Wendy turned and left his office, closing the door softly behind her.

Jared deliberately watched her go, then, as slowly as he could, he moved to the chair behind his desk and sat down. "What's the problem?" he asked, steepling his fingers before him.

"What's the problem?" she repeated incredulously. "The *problem,* I'm starting to realize, is *you.*"

"You're going to have to calm down and try to be a little more lucid," Jared said. "Why don't you take a seat? And maybe a few deep breaths."

"I don't need deep breaths, I need a new counselor. And maybe," she added ominously, "a lawyer."

Obviously there was some kind of weird misunderstanding going on here. "I don't have a clue what you're talking about," Jared said honestly. "Why don't you tell me the problem before we hire the big guns?"

"You honestly don't know what I'm upset about?" she asked, narrowing her eyes suspiciously.

"No."

"Some psychiatrist."

"Melanie, what the hell are ou going on about?"

"My 'date' with Tony, of course."

Oh, no. He knew he should have checked Tony out first. "Tony?" Jared assumed a blank expression.

"Tony Doddi." She crossed her arms in front of

her and all but tapped her toe on the floor. "Marvin's son. Ring a bell?"

"Oh, yes, Tony Doddi. The artist. Of course." He cleared his throat. "What's the matter with Tony?"

"Only that he showed up at my apartment last night for our appointment with a dozen red roses."

"And roses…make you angry? You're allergic?" Jared frowned and shook his head. "I'm afraid I'm not following."

"He thought it was a date, Jared. He was under the impression that you'd set us up on a date."

"Ah." Jared nodded, as if he was only now getting it. "Obviously we had a miscommunication about your meeting."

"Oh, I don't think so," Melanie said sharply. "I think you did it deliberately."

Mercifully, Wendy chose that moment to come back with the tea. She knocked once, then opened the door, no doubt hoping to catch some interesting tidbit.

"Here's your tea, Miss Tourbier."

Melanie didn't quite smile but she was at least gracious. "Thank you, Wendy. You really didn't have to trouble yourself." She set the tea down on the desk, where Jared was fairly certain it would remain untouched. "You really shouldn't have," she added, staring at Jared.

"Oh, it was no trouble." Wendy stood, unmoving.

"Thanks, Wendy," Jared said, without Melanie's polite control. "You can go now."

Wendy slunk out of the room.

"Now, you were saying…?" He hoped she'd forgotten what she was saying.

No such luck. "I was saying that I think you deliberately sent Tony Doddi over thinking we were going on a date."

"Why would I do that?"

"Because you are so determined that I shouldn't have artificial insemination that you've taken it upon yourself to set me up with eligible—if not desirable—men!"

"Nonsense," Jared said without much conviction. "I didn't say or imply to Tony that this was a date." Which was true. He hadn't talked to Tony at all. Marvin had arranged things on his end.

"Who did, then?"

"I have no idea. It sounds like it was just a misunderstanding. Certainly nothing for you to get so hot under the collar about. Did you go to dinner with him?"

"Oh, yes," she said. "We went to dinner. Fast-food burgers in his car at some remote point by the lake, which I can only guess, from the proliferation of teenager-filled cars around us, is the local make-out point."

Jared was stunned by the depth of Tony's stupidity. How could he think Melanie was the fast-food, make-out point type? What was he, an idiot? Anyone could see that Melanie was the type of woman you treated to champagne and lobster.

"You're sure this was Tony Doddi?" he asked.

"Oh, yes. Dark-haired fellow? About a foot shorter than I am and two feet wider?" She nodded, a wild glint in her eye. "It was Tony."

That didn't sound like the Tony whom Jared remembered. Granted Tony had been about fourteen the last time Jared had seen him, but he'd been a nice-looking kid. Jared had just assumed he'd grown. Up more than out. "I don't know what to tell you, Melanie, I'm really sorry. Were you, uh, able to talk about his art?"

"His *art?*" She repeated, then laughed. "Oh, yes, his *art* came up."

"What's so funny?" Jared wasn't sure he wanted to know.

"Tony," she said through a frozen false smile, "is a ventriloquist."

"A what?"

"A ventriloquist." She paced in front of his desk. "I guess I should have been more clear when we were talking about my parents' galleries that they're primarily interested in fine artists. You know, painters, sculptors, that sort of thing. They almost never display—" she gave him a venomous look "—puppets."

Jared couldn't help it, he laughed. "I had no idea. When his father said he was in the arts, I assumed...well, obviously, I had no idea he meant, um, the performing arts."

She sat heavily in the chair opposite him and sighed. "He's not even a good ventriloquist."

Jared could barely contain himself. "He gave you a demonstration?" It was fascinating in a horrible sort of way. "Did he actually bring the puppet with him?"

She raised an eyebrow and deadpanned, "Dingo tried to unhook my bra."

He was almost afraid to ask. "Dingo?"

She let out a long, overly patient breath, before explaining, "Yes, Dingo the Dummy."

That did it. Jared laughed until his empty stomach began to ache. "I didn't plan it that way, I swear," he finally told her.

She stood before him, her arms crossed in front of her, and waited for him to finish. "What I want to know," she said when he'd sobered some, "is *what* you're planning? Do you really think you can set me up with a man and stop me from having a baby alone?"

"Who said I'm trying to set you up with a man?"

"Oh, please. Do you think I'm an idiot? I'll admit, trying to set me up with a gay guy did throw me off the track at first—"

"Gay guy?"

"—but by last night, all the pieces fell into place and I figured out exactly what you were up to."

"Wait a minute. What gay guy?"

She looked at him incredulously. "Lance? Hello?"

"Lance is *gay?*"

Her mouth dropped open. "Are you joking?"

"No!"

Now it was her turn to look astonished. "How long have you known him?"

"A year or so." He thought about it. Yes, Lance had been very keen on getting those ballet tickets, and he did dress rather flamboyantly, but he'd come to Mission Creek from the West Coast. Jared had just assumed he was eccentric.

"And you're a psychiatrist?"

"I don't judge people."

She rolled her eyes. "Except me."

"I don't judge you, either," he argued. "I'm trying to help you."

She lifted her brows. "So you admit you were trying to set me up on dates with those guys!"

"I'll admit that I thought you might have something in common with them and that it wouldn't have been a bad thing if you'd hit it off."

"Well, that right there just shows how little you know me. I mean, if you were going to try to set me up with someone, why didn't you pick someone like Dr. Lewis?"

"Mark Lewis?"

"Mmm-hmm." She nodded, a small smug smile on her lips.

"You want to go out with Mark Lewis?" Jared asked sharply. Mark Lewis was a pediatrician on the fifth floor, and he was notorious for loving and leaving the nurses and any other female who came along and was bowled over by his looks and his swagger.

"What if I did?" she countered.

"He's all wrong for you!"

"Unlike the other two guys you picked, who are perfect for me?"

He still couldn't quite reconcile himself to the idea that Lance was gay, but he took her at her word. "However wrong they might be for you, it doesn't make Mark Lewis right for you."

She crossed her legs, taking easy control of the conversation. "No? Why not?"

"For one thing, he won't make a commitment."

"Maybe he just hasn't met the right woman."

"If he's read a book since college, I'd be surprised."

She shrugged. "I can live with that. I have a book group to talk about literature with."

Frustration rose in Jared like mercury on a thermometer. "He listens to county music."

Her eyes widened. "I love country music!" She smiled broadly. "This guy is sounding better and better. Can you introduce us?"

"No," Jared said sharply. He couldn't stand the idea of Mark Lewis driving Melanie around in his stupid Jeep, blasting music about lost dogs and trucks, while he rested his hand on her thigh....

It was Melanie's turn to laugh. "Wow, that's pretty vehement. I was only joking, but you take your matchmaking pretty seriously, don't you?"

"I've never done any matchmaking before in my life," Jared said honestly.

"So why now?" she asked, her voice softer. "Why me?"

It was a good question.

He didn't have a good answer.

He didn't even have a bad answer.

Why *was* he trying so hard to set Melanie up with a man? His original idea had been to solve the problem of approving her for fertility treatments, but that still begged the question of why he'd chosen guys who were so clearly inappropriate for her. She was right—he *was* a psychiatrist, for crying out loud. He should have known that Lance wasn't particularly interested in women. He'd never seen him with one. And he did talk a lot about his friend Perry, the synchronized swimmer who loved decorating.

Had Jared done it on purpose? Had he set her up with men he knew wouldn't or couldn't satisfy her because he didn't want her to fall in love with someone? Or, rather, with someone else?

The truth hit him like a ton of bricks. How had he been so blind to his own feelings? How had he denied them so completely? Melanie was right, had been all along. They did have a problem, a problem that would prevent him from making an objective evaluation of her case. There was only one thing he could do about it and he had to do it now.

"I apologize for all of his," he said, his voice gruff. "You're right, I—I've lost some objectivity."

"Well, I'm glad you can admit it," she said.

"Thank you. Now, will you stop trying to set me up on dates?"

"I'll do more than that," he said. "I'm going to remove myself from your case."

Her mouth dropped open. "What?"

"I'm going to find you another counselor."

Eight

Melanie was stunned. "You don't want to be my counselor anymore?" She knew darn well that she could go to Tabitha Monroe if she needed to and have him taken off the case, but it never even occurred to her that he might take himself off the case.

He looked pained. "Melanie, it's not that I don't want to be your counselor, it's just that, you're right, I've lost objectivity." He raked his hand through his hair. "Hell, maybe I never really had it."

Never had she been less satisfied to be right.

Granted, she and Jared Cross had certainly had their problems, but she thought they were making progress. Just the fact that he cared enough to try to set her up on dates—however misguided the impulse was—showed that he wasn't going to simply nix her candidacy.

The idea of starting over with a new therapist wasn't appealing at all.

"But, Jared," she said, "we may as well finish what we started. We've come this far."

"I'm not sure we've gotten anywhere."

Unsure of how to respond, she picked up the tea Wendy had brought in. It was still warm. She took a sip, then said, "Everyone says you're a great doctor, the consummate professional. Surely after our counseling sessions, you can see that—"

She never got to finish her sentence. Outside, an explosion rocked the building on its foundation. The noise echoed and rebounded in suspended time, seeming to go on forever. The window buzzed then cracked into a spiderweb pattern, as if someone had thrown a rock through it.

Melanie froze, the tea she was holding spilling unceremoniously down her front.

This is it, a voice inside her head screamed. *They've come to get you. You always knew it would happen. It's happening now. Say goodbye. This is the end. Goodbye.*

Images of her parents flooded through her mind. Scenes she had never replayed before rose from the depths of her subconscious, as fresh as if she had just woken from a deep sleep. The airport. Her mother, in a pale-blue dress, which Melanie had said made her look like Dorothy from *The Wizard of Oz*. The smell of Shalimar perfume in the air, mingling with her father's drugstore aftershave. Melanie still had the bottle somewhere, although it had probably turned to alcohol by now. Where was that? She needed to find it. He needed it back. She had to give it to him.

Suddenly his hand was on her back. "Be good while we're gone, peanut," he was saying. She'd forgotten that he called her peanut. How did she forget that? He'd done it for the first fifteen years of her life!

"What do you want from Paris?" he asked. "Some champagne? Perfume?"

"Oh, Doug," her mother had said, smiling at her. "Don't make my baby grow up too fast. I bet you want one of those puppets from Gepetto's, don't you, sweetheart?"

She did. She wanted the gypsy marionette that had a black silk dress with red flowers on it.

"I know just the one," her mother said with a wink.

A muffled voice. Last boarding call. Time to go. Goodbye.

"Bye, peanut." Her dad kissed the top of her head. She touched him. For hours afterward she could smell the aftershave on her fingertips.

"We'll see you in a few days," her mother said, kissing her cheek. "Oh, no, I got lipstick on you." She rubbed it off with her thumb. Melanie could still feel the spot. "Goodbye!" Waving, happy, excited about a romantic weekend for just the two of them. "See you on Tuesday."

But Tuesday never came. At least the Tuesday in which they came back home and everything was normal. The plane had exploded one hour and 46 minutes after takeoff, sending fuselage and metal downward and souls upward. When she got the news, Melanie could still smell her father's scent, and could still feel her mother's touch.

"...Melanie!" The voice was urgent. She felt

hands on her, shaking her gently. "It's okay, Melanie, you're okay."

She closed her heavy eyelids, blinked once, then twice before focusing on the man before her. Jared Cross. His green eyes were as warm and deep as a lake. She wanted to dive in. Something told her it was safe in there.

"Melanie?" he repeated.

"Yes." Her mouth felt dry.

"We have to get out of here. They're evacuating the building."

"Yes." She couldn't move. Her limbs were as heavy as lead.

"Melanie," he tried again, then she heard him expel a breath and say "hold on."

Next thing she knew, she was being swept into powerful arms and carried away. She saw herself and Jared Cross as if from a point some distance away. The weak female saved by the strong male. She should get down, walk on her own two feet, only at the moment she couldn't seem to feel her own two feet, much less use them.

"Is she okay?" she heard a voice ask, but she couldn't see who was asking. Her eyelids were too heavy. She'd just close her eyes for a moment. That would make everything go away.

"What happened?" another voice asked.

"She'll be fine." It was Jared. Confident. Capable. Of course she'd be fine. She'd been fine for fifteen years on her own. "I can walk myself," she murmured.

"No way. You've had a shock. I'm not going to risk you falling down the stairwell."

She licked her parched lips. "I won't fall."

"Damn right you won't."

It was hard to say how much time had passed. Maybe five minutes, maybe an hour, but when they got outside, the sun hit Melanie like a slap in the face. She struggled down from Jared's arms and tried to smooth her clothing, but her legs felt weak.

"Whoa, there," he said, catching her when she lost her balance.

"I'm sorry about that." She gestured toward the building. "I don't know what happened to me."

"I do," he said gently. "It's a form of post-traumatic stress syndrome."

She tried to shake the cobwebs from her head. "Why? I've never been through anything like this."

"Your parents," he said, his arm steadying her. "You talked about your parents."

She swallowed. "I did?"

"Yes." He didn't say anything more. What could he say?

Gradually Melanie became aware of the crowd around them. "What happened?"

"I'm not sure." Jared tapped the shoulder of a doctor who was standing nearby. "Any idea what blew?" he asked.

The woman shrugged. "Might have been the gas line. They're not sure yet."

"Where was it?"

"Right outside the nursery window."

"The nursery!" Melanie exclaimed. "Oh, my God! Was anyone—" She couldn't finish.

The doctor shook her head. "No one was hurt."

Melanie's shoulders sagged with relief. "Thank goodness." She shuddered at the thought of what might have been.

Jared's arm tightened around her shoulder. "I think we'd better get you home. This has all been a bit much for you."

"No more than anyone else," Melanie protested, ashamed of how weak she felt.

He led her away from the crowd, toward his car. "As a matter of fact, I think this *is* more difficult for you than for most people, and with good reason. You've had a hell of a shock, and that's nothing to be embarrassed about."

Tears burned in her eyes. "You're very kind."

He smiled, though there was tension still etched in his face. "Is this really Melanie Tourbier, telling me I'm kind?"

"Funny, I was wondering if it was really you," she said, smiling only for a moment. "Seriously, Jared, I do appreciate this."

"It's nothing." He felt in his pocket for his keys. "I'm going to drive you home. You definitely can't go out on the road in this condition."

"I'm fine."

"You will be, but you're not driving."

She didn't argue. She wasn't all that eager to get behind the wheel anyway. As a matter of fact, she wasn't all that eager to be alone. She was glad to have at least a few more minutes with Jared so that she wouldn't have to face her demons again. As long as she was with him, she felt safe.

They made their way to his car and he helped her into the passenger seat. "This really isn't necessary," she said. "I'm not ill."

He smiled. "Come on, it's not that often I get to be a gentleman. I need the practice."

"Don't you have a girlfriend to practice on?" Melanie asked, wondering why she cared if he had a girlfriend or not. Her interest in him certainly wasn't personal. Still, she waited with bated breath for his answer.

"Nope," he said, closing the door behind her and walking around the front of the car to his door.

She watched him walk. He had a nice gait, graceful but masculine. You could tell there was power underneath his work clothes.

"No girlfriend?" she heard herself ask after he'd closed his door and started the car.

He glanced over at her, amusement in his green eyes. "You're not going to try to set me up with someone, are you?"

"It would serve you right," she said, crossing her

arms in front of her. "Maybe a sweet little old lady from Peoria. Or a nun."

"Okay, okay, I get the point." He tapped his fingers on the steering wheel. "Mea culpa. I'll never try matchmaking again."

"That's good news for all the women of the world."

"My intentions were good."

"Maybe. But your taste is deplorable."

"Hey, a lot of people enjoy a good ventriloquist act."

"Then I hope those people don't go see Tony Doddi, because they'll be sorely disappointed."

Jared laughed.

It felt good to finally be having a civil conversation with him. He was a good guy, it turned out. Tabitha and Em were right about him. His facade was certainly stern but underneath it all, Jared Cross had a sense of humor and an unexpected sense of compassion. As a matter of fact, that, combined with his strength and intelligence, made him a very good package all around. Some woman would be very lucky to win him over someday.

In the meantime, Melanie just needed to win him over enough for him to stay on her case and approve her plan to have a baby. She needed to stay focused on that objective.

"Do you think it's possible that someone created that explosion on purpose?" Melanie asked after a few minutes of silence.

A muscle ticked in Jared's jaw and for a moment he didn't say anything. When he spoke, his voice was hard. "I hope not."

"But you think it's possible."

"Yes, I do."

"That's what I thought." It was a bomb. Every instinct in her said it was a bomb.

"Look, don't worry about that right now. The authorities are on the scene and they'll find out what's going on. You need to take care of yourself." He glanced at her chest, then looked away quickly. "Maybe get some fresh clothes."

"What?" She touched the spot where he'd looked and realized that her entire blouse was soaking and somewhat transparent. "Oh, I completely forgot about the tea."

"I'm afraid your shirt is ruined."

"I can wash it. I guess I'm lucky that it was only tea."

"That's true." He pulled the car into her parking lot. "Should I drive to the front or the back of your building?"

"The back. I usually go to the back." But suddenly she didn't want to go at all. She didn't want to go into her apartment, alone with her ghosts. Inexplicable panic swept over her in an icy wave.

"You got it," Jared said, looking at the road and therefore oblivious of the mini nervous breakdown she seemed to be having in the seat next to him. He pulled into a space and put the car in park. "I'll walk you up—'' he started to say, then stopped. "Melanie? Are you okay?"

"Yes, why?"

"You're white as a sheet."

"I—I—" She raised a shaking hand to her hair. "I'm sorry, I don't know what's wrong with me...." Her entire body trembled.

"Are you ill?"

"No, just..." She gave a feeble smile. "I don't want to be alone."

"Oh." His entire expression softened. "I should have realized that." He hesitated, as if considering options.

"This is stupid," Melanie said after a moment. "I'm a grown woman. I can go to my apartment alone."

He didn't agree. "Look, why don't you come back with me to my place?"

"Your place?" she repeated, surprised.

He shrugged. "Well, I'd take you back to my office, but it's been closed for the time being."

"I really don't want to impose," she said, suddenly getting a peculiar feeling in the pit of her stomach. Warming up to him in a professional context was one thing, but getting cozy in his apartment was quite another.

"It's no imposition. In fact, I don't really see an alternative, since it would be irresponsible for me to leave you alone at your place right now and there's nowhere else for you to go."

"When did I become a charity case?"

"You're not a charity case," he said.

"I certainly feel like one."

"Melanie, I care about you, okay? Come with me because I care." He looked at her plaintively. "Please."

A lump rose in her throat. "Really?"

He nodded. "Really."

She smiled. "In that case, I guess I really shouldn't let you down."

"Good girl." He started the car again and put it in gear. "I'll give you some dry clothes and throw yours into the washer."

An hour later, Melanie was comfortably installed on Jared's sofa, wrapped in a fluffy white terry bathrobe, which had been a gift from a former girlfriend who had somehow envisioned him as a fluffy white terry-cloth robe kind of guy.

He'd had to take the tags off before handing it to Melanie.

"How are you feeling?" he asked, bringing her a cup of coffee from the kitchen. It wasn't the most soothing drink, but it was all he had. At least it was decaf.

"Better," she said, taking the cup. "Thanks." She sipped slowly and smiled. "That's good."

"I'm an ace cook when it comes to mixing dehydrated coffee powder into hot water."

"The trick is to get just the right proportion. Not everyone can do that."

He laughed and sat down on the chair next to the couch. "I straightened the bedroom up a little. Why don't you just stay here for the night? I'll sleep on the couch," he hastened to add.

"That's way above and beyond the call of duty," Melanie said. "You shouldn't have to baby-sit me all night."

"Frankly, the prospect has its appeal," he said, before he could stop himself. "I mean, it's the best way for me to insure that you're really okay tonight." What had he said? Worse, what had he *meant?* He fully intended to remove himself from Melanie's case but since he hadn't done it yet, technically he was still her counselor. And for her counselor to be having such inappropriate thoughts about her was just... wrong.

"You take your work seriously, don't you?" Melanie mused aloud.

"Yes, very."

"Then don't let go of me."

That caught him off guard. "What?"

"Don't drop my case." She set her coffee down and leaned forward, holding the robe together with one hand. "Jared, you've delved into the darkest depths of my psyche and examined me inside and out. I've confided things to you that I've never confided to another human being." There were tears shining in her eyes. "Surely you know enough to know I'd be a good mother."

"I have little doubt of that."

Hope lit her smile. "Does that mean you'll recommend me for the treatment?"

"It means I'll recommend you to another counselor who can make an objective determination."

She leaned back and sighed. "I don't think I can go through all of that again."

"Opening yourself up can only be good for you."

She gave a humorless laugh. "Easy for you to say. Have you ever opened up to anyone in your life?"

Not since he was a child, too young to know better. "What I've done is not the point."

"Aha!" She pointed a finger at him. "I'll take that as a no."

"I didn't say yes or no."

"You didn't have to." She looked into his eyes. "You also don't have to say there's a lot under the surface there that needs to come out."

"Now you're the doctor?"

"It doesn't take a doctor to see that."

"I'll keep that in mind."

She considered him for a moment, then said, "You really are haunted by something, aren't you?"

"What on earth makes you say that?"

"I don't know exactly." She sipped her coffee and set the cup down. "Something in your eyes. You know when I really see it?"

He swallowed visibly. "No, when?"

"Whenever you talk about how horrible it is for children to feel unwanted by their parents."

He didn't answer.

"Did you feel unwanted, Jared? Is that why you work so hard to make sure it doesn't happen to someone else?"

He let out a long breath, then said, "You don't want to know my sordid history."

"Yes, I do," she said seriously. "If you're willing to tell me, I'd like very much to know about you."

He picked up his coffee mug and held it with two hands. A muscle ticked in his clenched jaw for a moment, then he said, "There isn't much to tell. I never knew my father and I barely knew my mother."

"She was gone a lot?"

"When I was with her, she was gone a lot, yes. Then she left me at an orphanage when I was three."

Melanie's heart constricted. "Oh, no. I had no idea."

He looked hard, rather than sad. "It's nothing for you to get sentimental about. I'm not."

"Jared, it's heartbreaking. Why did she leave you there? Do you know?"

"My memory is patchy, but I'm pretty sure it was because I cramped her dating style." He gave a dry laugh. "I don't mean that to sound so bitter, but I remember men. Lots of different men. Couldn't tell you even one of their names, but I remember lying in the dark in my room and hearing her in her room. Sometimes it was laughter, sometimes it was yelling, sometimes it was hard to tell. Always it was frightening.''

Melanie tried to swallow, but her throat felt tight and dry. "That's so very sad. And unfair.''

He shrugged. "The only part that was really unfair was that she waited so long to take me to the orphanage. By the time a child is beyond the baby stage, he's no longer so attractive to prospective parents.''

She shook her head. "I don't know how they turn down any of the children." She shifted her weight and thought before admitting, "I tried to adopt, you know. In London. They wouldn't let me because I was single.''

Jared looked up, surprised. "You tried to adopt?''

"Sure. It was the first logical step, I thought. But they didn't want to have the children going into the uncertainty of a single parent home. That's what they said anyway. I think the truth was that they believed the same stories you read, and believed them enough to think a child was better off in an orphanage than living with a wanton woman like me.''

Jared's green eyes blazed. "Whoever was in charge of that decision should be fired.''

She raised an eyebrow. "Really? How different is that from what's happening here?''

"A lot. There's a world of difference between giving a home to a child who doesn't have one and bringing a child into the world under less than optimal conditions. Not that I'm saying you have less than optimal conditions, you understand.''

"I understand," she said, then sighed. "Funny after going through the nightmare of trying to adopt, I thought this was going to be the easier way. I figured if it was my baby, no one could tell me I wasn't qualified to give him or her a home."

"I'm sorry if I've made this hard on you."

"What would really make it hard is if I had to start all over with a new counselor. I don't think I can go through it all again. I don't think I can afford to lose that much more time."

"The time shouldn't matter."

"Of course the time matters," she said with quiet force. "I'm already thirty. I'll be thirty-one in two months. You know how hard it will be for me to get pregnant, you know how long it could take. The risks for normal women increase with every year. For me," her voice wavered, "it's a one in a million shot. My odds of winning the lottery are better. Please, Jared, *please* stay on the case." The tears flowed freely now, spilling down her cheeks and onto the thick terry robe.

"Don't cry," Jared said, moving over to her. "Everything will work out for the best, I promise."

She sniffed. "How can you promise that? Look at all the preconceptions you had about me. The next person might have twice as many. I'll never have a family. It's the one thing that's meant the most in my life and it's the one thing I can never have."

Professionalism be damned, he took her in his arms. "Don't cry," he whispered.

She pulled back. "I can't help it."

He cupped her face with his hands and brushed the tears away with his thumbs. "I hate to see you so sad."

"I'm sorry." Her lower lip trembled. "This isn't just about me. It's everything. It's what you just told me, it's the explosion, it's my parents. It's probably a lack of sleep, too, because I'm not usually so weak."

"It's not weak to show emotion."

"It's not strong, either." She sniffed. "Please don't drop my case, Jared. Please."

He cupped her cheek. "Can't you see that I've lost my objectivity? You don't want a guy with feelings for you to make a decision that might affect the rest of your life."

"Feelings?" she repeated, the tears still filling her eyes.

He nodded. "Melanie, right now I'd do anything to bring a smile back to your face. Believe me, you don't want me to encourage you to move forward with your plan just because I don't want you to cry."

She pressed her lips together and closed her eyes, then nodded. "You're right. You're absolutely right." Her shoulders sagged. "What do we do?" Her blue eyes were pools of emotion. "What now?"

"I'll keep the case," he said, against his better judgment. "You won't have to start the whole process over again."

"Thank you," she said through her tears. "I feel like such an idiot blubbering like this."

"No," he said gently, wiping a tear from her cheek. "Don't." Wordlessly he bent down and lowered his mouth onto hers.

His lips grazed lightly across hers at first. Melanie leaned into him and for a moment, they were still, their breath mingling between them. Then Jared's mouth found hers again, but this time it was hungrier, more insistent. His tongue touched hers and a jolt of desire shuddered through her.

She traced her hands up his arms and pulled him closer to her, eagerly exploring his mouth with her own.

Jared ran a strong hand down to the small of Melanie's back. A tingle of excitement arched Melanie's back, catlike.

A pulse throbbed in her core, willing him, like a hypnotic drum, to keep going, to keep touching her.

As if he understood, Jared slipped his hands under her shirt and along the bare skin above her bra. Melanie's breath caught in her throat. She responded with the force of desire too long denied.

She wanted him.

As Jared's lips moved against hers and his tongue probed gently in her mouth, Melanie faced a longing deeper than any she'd ever felt. It wasn't just physical, it was emotional. It was spiritual.

It was *need*.

Letting go of her inhibitions, Melanie reached for

the button fly of Jared's khaki pants and twisted the buttons free, one by one, with controlled deliberation.

He edged closer to her, increasing the urgency of his kisses.

She tugged his pants down over his narrow hips and slid her hand down behind the waistband of his briefs. He was already ready for her, a fact that made her tingle between her legs.

She pulled the briefs down, her fervor increasing with every moment as she grew frantic to have him within her. Their tongues moved against each other in the frenzied rhythm of what was to come.

Jared unbuttoned Melanie's shirt and slipped it off her, holding her gaze with his own. Then he slipped her bra off in one smooth move and tossed it aside, as if she'd never have need of it again. As if they were going to spend the rest of their lives here, naked, locked together in a hungry embrace. By the time he unfastened the top button of her pants, her need was so powerful, she could barely get out of them fast enough. The fabric slid across the tops of her thighs, leaving a tingling trail behind.

Smiling against her mouth, Jared slipped his arm around Melanie's back and lowered her into the sofa. The cushions felt cool beneath her back. She imagined she could hear a sizzle as her hot skin met the cool.

His hand brushed her lower belly and hooked in the damp crotch of her panties. There was only a second's hesitation before he gave one long pull, separating the thin cotton away from the spot he sought. Melanie felt her nails pushing into his back and heard her own ragged gasps as his hands worked magically on her until the dizzying waves of pleasure she felt reached a crest and she parted her legs in open invitation.

Slowly Jared lowered the whole of his weight on her, momentarily pressing the breath from her lungs. She opened her mouth and allowed his kisses to deepen, satiating a thirst she had not realized before.

He burrowed his hands into her hair and kissed her face, her neck, her lips, then, in one smooth motion, he entered her.

He drew out slowly and she watched as he crossed the room and retrieved a condom.

It was on the tip of her tongue to make a joke about how obviously unnecessary that was, but this was definitely not the time for joking. He was clearly taking a doctorly approach to caution and she couldn't fault him for that.

A moment later, when he laid his warmth on her again and reentered her, she forgot all about it. They both moaned in pleasure as her body accepted his, and they moved together, slowly at first, and then faster until she heard him hold his breath for a moment then give one final thrust. She felt herself glide into ecstasy.

This was lovemaking as she'd never known it before. She felt completely fulfilled, completely satisfied. Now, at long last, she knew what people meant when they said it was right.

This was right.

Yet as she drifted off to sleep, her head on Jared's chest, listening to the steady thumping of his heart as he traced his fingertips up and down her back, something in her was afraid. Some small voice warned her that love never worked out for her.

And it never would.

Nine

Melanie opened her eyes to blaring sunshine. For a moment, she couldn't figure out where she was. Her bedroom didn't face the east. If she didn't raise the shade, it would be dark until afternoon.

Then she remembered.

She was in Jared Cross's apartment.

For one delicious moment she replayed the evening's events, savoring the memory of his first kisses and the power of his lovemaking.

Then she remembered the vague sense of unease she'd had afterward, and the same feeling returned to her.

But that was just silly paranoia. Wasn't it?

She turned over and looked at the man still sleeping next to her, the sunlight playing across his strong shoulder and lighting his tousled dark hair. He was gorgeous. No two ways about it. And he'd wanted her, there was no doubt. The passion he'd shown had been breathtaking. Surely something that felt that good couldn't be wrong.

She laid a hand on his arm and he stirred.

"Hey," she said softly.

He rolled toward her and opened sleepy eyes. As soon as he saw her, he smiled.

Her heart tripped.

"You were in my dream," he said. "Or am I dreaming now?"

"That was no dream, Doctor, and neither is this."

He grinned. "So the aliens landing at the country club to take you back to their home planet were real?"

She pursed her lips. "That's the best dream about me that you could come up with? An alien abduction?"

He laughed and threw an arm across her, pulling her close. "I like reality better."

"Me, too." She was about to kiss him when his watched beeped. "What's that?"

He looked at his watch, then groaned. "We overslept."

"What?"

He clicked his tongue against his teeth. "I have an appointment in twenty-five minutes." He threw the covers back, then stopped and, like the gentleman he was, replaced enough so that she wasn't exposed.

"It's a little late for modesty, don't you think?" Melanie asked, letting the covers drop off her naked form.

"Old habits," he said with a quick grin and an appreciative sweep of a gaze before he hurried into the bathroom for a shower.

Meanwhile, Melanie got out of bed, took a brush

from her purse and pulled her hair back, and put on her clothes from yesterday. Hopefully no one would recognize them.

Jared came out of the bathroom with a towel slung around his hips. Melanie couldn't help but admire his physique in the daylight. He was muscular but lean. Every movement suggested a quiet power that she found simply irresistible.

"I was going to ask if you wanted me to send a cab for you in a bit, but you've managed to pull yourself together faster than me," Jared said, tossing the towel aside and getting dressed.

Melanie's heart thrummed as she watched his muscles flex subtly with his movements. "I'm ready when you are."

He tucked his shirt in and sat down on the edge of the bed to put on his shoes and socks. "There's going to be talk if anyone notices us coming in together," he warned.

She shrugged. "If people are talking about anything other than the explosion, I'll be amazed."

"Don't underestimate Mission Creek's interest in gossip." He stood up and hastily straightened his clothes. "There's room for more than one story in this town. You ready?"

"Yup."

"Let's go. The hospital cafeteria makes a decent cup of coffee, if you're interested. Or do you want to go home and change your clothes before you go to the hospital?"

The mention of going home made Melanie's adrenaline surge. She had to go home sometime, she supposed. It might as well be sooner rather than later. "I think I will," she said with false courage. "You can drop me off at my car and I'll go back and change."

He stopped, evidently hearing the uncertainty she'd tried so hard to keep from her voice. "Look, if you don't want to go back alone—"

"It's okay," she said firmly. "No problem."

"You sure?"

She nodded and walked with him to the front door. "Absolutely. I've been taking care of myself for fifteen years. I'm pretty sure I can go back to my apartment and change my clothes alone."

"I'd be glad to help you with that," he said, giving a wolfish smile. "But I'm afraid it would make me late."

"When's your appointment?"

He looked at his watch again and muttered an oath. "Ten minutes. I think I can just make it."

They hurried out to his car and started toward the hospital.

"I'll talk to Tabitha this morning about getting you a new counselor," Jared said, pulling into the light traffic on Mission Creek Drive.

Melanie felt as if she'd been punched in the stomach. "*What?* I thought you were going to stay on the job."

He glanced at her sideways. "After last night I really don't think that's appropriate, do you?"

"What has last night got to do with your professional assessment of me as a person?" Melanie wanted to know. "If anything, I would think it proves that you realize I'm a good person."

"A cynic might say it proves that I think you're an *attractive* person."

She blinked. "Is that what last night was all about? Physical attraction?"

"There was definitely physical attraction."

"But is that all?" Her heart sank. She'd done it again, gotten involved with a man who wanted something from her other than her heart. If it wasn't money, it was sex. She should be used to it by now.

"No, it's not all," he said simply. "Not by a long shot." He reached over and covered her hand with his for a moment. "Which is all the more reason I shouldn't be your counselor."

She found that heartening although frustrating. "Jared, does having sex prevent you from doing your job properly?"

"In general? No."

"Then why would it in this case? Yes, we made love." Her heart pounded, remembering. "And it was wonderful. But did it change who we were beforehand? Last night you agreed that I'd be a good mom."

"I still think you'd be a great mom," he said simply. "The question is whether you'd be a great *single* mom."

She sighed. "And...?"

He hesitated. "And that's what I was in the process of determining when...well, last night happened." He turned the car into the Mission Creek Hospital grounds.

Melanie knew she had to act fast, to persuade him to at least postpone his decision so he didn't talk to Tabitha yet. "You have strong opinions about children, Jared, and I admire that. And I understand something of why you feel that way. But I think you know, in your heart, that I'm ready for this and that it would be a positive move for both me and, more importantly, the baby." She paused before adding, "You've said yourself that the world needs more caring and loving parents."

"That's true," he conceded.

"So if you pass my case along to someone else, what happens if they have the same prejudice against me that you did in the beginning? What if the new counselor can't or won't see past the headlines?"

Jared parked and put the car in gear, then turned to face Melanie. "I see your point. Let me think about it, okay?"

"Okay," she said, not because she agreed so much as she didn't see a choice.

"Are you free for lunch?"

Every day. "Yes."

"I'll pick you up at noon. We'll go to the cafeteria and talk."

"All right," she agreed, trepidation filling her every pore. "I'll see you at noon."

* * *

Going home proved to be anticlimactic for Melanie.

After everything that had happened over the past eighteen hours, she was so full of conflicting emotions that they all seemed to cancel each other out.

Except her feelings for Jared. While they weren't exactly clear, they were most definitely strong.

She'd found him attractive the moment she'd met him, of course. After vowing to Jeff, and anyone else who would listen, that she'd never even *look* at a man again, she'd surprised herself by feeling attracted to the tall, dark-haired stranger who had gotten on the elevator with her.

Of course, that had disappeared quickly when she'd learned he was her counselor and, moreover, that he was trying to counsel her *out* of having a baby. But as the days passed, she'd developed a grudging admiration for the man that had turned into something more.

She'd started to realize it when they'd gone to the Empire Room and Jared had ordered her father's special reserve wine. Her feelings had grown stronger still when he'd spoken so tenderly to her about her parents and about her dream of having a family and a home. He shared that dream, she could tell, even though he was reluctant to talk about himself.

She could also tell that he was on her side now. If only he would keep her case, she was confident he'd give the green light for her fertility treatments.

So he just *had* to keep her case.

Melanie went back to the hospital, unsure of what she'd find. To her relief, everything was up and running again, although there was a heavier police presence now than there had been before.

Melanie had to submit to a security check before entering the building, so she was five minutes late when she got to the day-care center.

"What's going on?" she asked Em after she'd put her purse in the back room. "Do they know what happened yet?"

Em nodded and spoke in a very low voice. "Someone set off a bomb outside the nursery window. Not a very sophisticated bomb, but if anyone had been close to it, they could have gotten badly hurt."

"Who would do such a thing? And why?"

"They suspect it was Branson Hines," Em said. "But so far they're not sure."

Melanie gasped. "Branson Hines! I thought he'd gone to Mexico!"

Em shrugged. "No one knows exactly where he is. Not even his wife, if her tearful pleas on television are to be believed."

"Sounds like you don't believe them."

"I just get an odd feeling about those two," Em said, shaking her head. "Of course, it's hard to say how much that has to do with what I know about them. Like his being accused of murder and getting off on a technicality."

"I put a lot of stock in instinct."

Em nodded. "I do, too, Melanie. And my instincts tell me this isn't over yet."

"I hope you're wrong," Melanie said, but she had the bad feeling that Em was right.

They were interrupted by a group of children, asking them to take the Candyland game off the shelf and play with them. Although Melanie would have liked to learn more about the bombing, she knew it wouldn't benefit her to relive the details. She knew also that a game or two of Candyland would do her some good. So she spent the rest of the morning playing it over and over until she practically had every card memorized.

Jared showed up at noon on the dot. As they walked to the cafeteria, his expression was considerably less open to Melanie than it had been in the morning, and she wondered if that was because of his work or her. If it was because of her, she figured she'd find out soon.

It was.

"We shouldn't have slept together last night," he said once they sat down at a table. "I should have been more professional and I apologize for putting you into such an awkward position."

"Which position are you thinking of?" she asked with a smile. "I don't remember feeling particularly awkward." His face remained serious and she stopped smiling. "At least not until right now."

"I'm sorry, Melanie. I know better than to get involved with a patient. I don't know what got into me.''

"Jared, it wasn't just you, you know. It was us. And, frankly, I don't have any regrets.''

His expression softened. "All right, to tell you the truth, I find it hard to say I have regrets about it myself.''

"I'm glad to hear that.'' She wanted to reach out and put her hand on his, but she knew it wasn't a good idea. "Then I don't see the problem.''

"The problem is it was still wrong and, more to the point right now, it would be wrong for us to do it again. I can't be your lover and your therapist at the same time. I'm sure you can understand that.''

It was black-and-white. She could understand it. "So which role are you proposing to give up?''

"We don't have any choice,'' he said, staring at his coffee as he stirred it aimlessly. "You don't want me off your case, so we can't have a relationship.''

"We can't?''

"No.''

"So it's only up to you and that's your decision?'' She snapped her fingers. "Just like that?''

"It's not an easy decision.''

"Nor is it a fair one,'' she countered. "Last night was one of the most…magical nights of my life. I hate to be cliché, but it's true. And I'd venture to say it was pretty special for you, too.''

He looked deeply into her eyes. "More than I can say.''

"So after that, you come in, think about it for three hours—while seeing other patients, by the way—and decide it's a no-go? And that's that?"

He took a deep breath, held it for a moment, then expelled it. "I did a little investigating this morning to find out who would be assigned to your case if I left it." He tapped his fingertips on the table and didn't meet Melanie's eyes. "Dr. Amanda Lundquist has turned down more than fifty percent of the applicants she's counseled, sometimes for reasons that I'd characterize as arbitrary."

Melanie felt herself deflate like a sunken soufflé. "And if she takes my case, you think she'll turn me down without even giving me a chance."

He nodded grimly. "If I were a betting man, I'd bet the farm *and* the ranch on it."

Her heart ached. If the choice was between a baby and a relationship with a man, there was no choice. She'd had enough relationships to know that they didn't work out for her. Ever. And while her night with Jared had been one of the most incredible experiences she'd ever had, she was smart enough now—or maybe jaded enough—to know that great sex was sometimes just that, great sex. It wasn't a guarantee of a great relationship.

She tried to swallow but there was a lump in her throat. "Does this mean you've made a decision about me?"

"It means I'm close to making a decision. I'd just like to meet with you a couple more times and make sure I've done all I can to help." He gave a small, apologetic smile. "Believe it or not, that really is what I've wanted all along. To help."

"I believe you." Tears pricked her eyes and she blinked them away. "I just wish things were different."

"So do I."

"What about…later?" She didn't dare say *after I have the baby*. She didn't want to jinx herself. "Do you think we might have a chance later?"

"I've thought about that. I just don't have an answer. Part of me says the hell with it, you only live once, but another part of me understands there would always be a shadow across our relationship. People would wonder if I'd made an objective opinion or if I was just trying to make you happy."

"Who cares what other people think?"

He gave a sad smile. "Okay, I'd wonder myself. If I approach this decision with the idea that you and I have a future, how can my decision not reflect that?"

"I see."

A moment passed.

"I'll be totally honest with you, Melanie. I haven't had good luck with relationships in the past. I just don't think I'm the relationship kind."

"I would have said the same thing about myself a few weeks ago," she agreed.

"And now?"

She looked at him and her chest felt tight. Her hands ached to touch him. "Now I don't know."

He looked pained. "Listen, I can't give you what you need. I can't give you the kind of—" he searched for the word "—intimacy you deserve. It's just a defect in my personality."

"Maybe you haven't met the right woman."

"Or maybe I have, but I'm too..." His voice trailed off. "I'm sorry. But I'm sure this is best for you."

She nodded, although she didn't agree. She wasn't going to argue with him right now, as it was obvious it would be fruitless. He'd made his decision about being with her. He didn't want to. He didn't want her. How could she argue with that?

Instead she would keep her focus on what was really important to her—having a baby. Starting a family.

Jared put his hands down on the table. "I have an appointment in a few minutes so I'm going to go."

"Now?" She didn't believe him. He was simply trying to get away from what was obviously an uncomfortable conversation. Who could blame him? "What about our appointment later? Is that still on?"

"Of course," he said, all business.

"Then I'll see you at the end of the day," she said, matching his clipped tone with one of her own. "If you'll excuse me, I'd better get back to the day-care center." She stood up and left, leaving her bagel and coffee untouched.

* * *

"For this session, I want to take a slightly different approach to things," Jared said after hours that night in his office.

"That's sounds daunting," Melanie answered.

"No, not at all. I think we know each other well enough now to drop the formality and just talk frankly to each other."

She nodded. "I think you're right. And if it will move my case forward, I'm all for it."

"Good." His gaze lingered on her eyes for a moment longer than usual. "I also think it's best if we try to act as though...well, you know, as though the other night never happened."

"I agree."

"Good." He looked at his hands. "So. Let's move beyond the should you–shouldn't you stage and talk about some of the basic practicalities of life as a single parent."

She straightened in her chair, readying herself for his questions like a clown readying himself for a pie in the face. "Okay, shoot."

He proceeded to ask her some basic questions about things like taking care of an infant alone when she'd only had two hours of sleep for several days in a row, and what she would do if the baby got ill in the middle of the night and so on. Things she'd already thought about a thousand times and had ready answers for.

But she wasn't ready for all of his questions.

"Moving on," Jared said, leaning back in his chair and studying Melanie. "What about when the child reaches elementary school age and begins to wonder why he or she doesn't have a dad. Have you thought about what your answer to that might be?"

"Well, I think I'll be honest about that from the beginning, so it never really comes up as a new question." There. It was a good answer, she thought. Especially considering it was off-the-cuff.

"It will come up," he said, shooting her confidence down. "On back-to-school night, on field trips, at times when other kids are making cards for their dads. A child who doesn't have a parent, be it a mother or father, becomes painfully aware of that fact during the elementary years."

"But a lot of kids lose a parent to divorce."

"It's different. An absent parent still exists. Most of the time, that parent is still part of the child's life, even if it's in a reduced capacity."

"What about children who lose a parent to death?"

"It's unfortunate but it does happen," he acknowledged. "And it's an extremely painful thing. But unlike the woman who loses her husband unexpectedly, you have the chance to make this decision in advance."

"It sounds as if you're trying to talk me out of this again," Melanie said suspiciously.

"No," he said quickly. "I'm simply trying to make you understand that the impact of this decision is far-reaching."

"Yes, of course it is." In her mind, she'd only added up the positives. She saw piano recitals, Christmas plays, graduations. She'd even envisioned her eventual grandmotherhood. But, she realized now, she'd only thought about the good stuff.

He continued to ask questions and pose theoretical situations and problems for her to solve. She answered each one without revealing her crumbling confidence. It was probably just a momentary lapse, she thought, and when she was able to go home and reflect on it, she was sure her enthusiasm and energy for the whole thing would return.

She was sure of it.

Every one of Melanie's answers had been a good one, Jared thought after she'd left. Although it was clear she hadn't given as much thought to the later part of childhood as she had to babyhood, her improvisation was impressive. In fact, it was far more telling than her rehearsed or oft-repeated answers from their past sessions ever had been.

At this point, he felt he knew her well enough to give an answer to the clinic. In fact, he'd known his answer for a while. He just wanted to be sure it was an honest, objective conclusion, not one colored by his personal feelings for and about her.

Because God knows his feelings were clouded. That night he'd spent with her had been incredible. Never had he known a woman more passionate, more giving, more open. He'd wanted it to go on forever.

Even in the morning, his first thoughts had been of seeing her again, of forging a future with her.

Of course, he'd quickly realized that was a foolish idea. Long ago he'd vowed never to get involved in another personal relationship, and so far that vow had served him in good stead. Why tinker with success?

Especially with a woman who lived thousands of miles away, on a different continent. Melanie Tourbier's home was in London, not the U.S. and certainly not in tiny Mission Creek, Texas.

Jared had been to London several times; he knew how different it was there. He knew that someone who loved the bustle and excitement of the big city could never possibly be happy in a small western town like Mission Creek, where everyone knew everyone else and the shops were closed on Sundays and dinner out meant going to one of about three decent places within a fifty-mile range.

It figured that he'd fall for a woman like that.

As a matter of fact, he wondered if subconsciously it really *did* figure. Perhaps he'd intentionally chosen a woman he could never have.

That was probably it.

His feelings weren't *real*, they were just his mind's way of excusing himself from having a relationship. Melanie was a convenient object of his imaginary affections. Nothing more.

Which was not to say it would be easy to let her go. But he knew enough to know that he had to do

. And he had to do it quickly and cleanly. Like pulling off a bandage.

His course was clear: the first step was to close the case on her. He was ready to do that. Personally, he thought she was setting herself up for a difficult twenty years or so, raising a child on her own, but he also thought she was up to the task. She'd been right when she said in the beginning that a child would be lucky to have a mother like her to love him.

Jared was confident that she was not only loving but capable and wise enough to make the right decisions, even when they had to be made quickly. Her instincts were excellent, he was glad to note. A lot of his questions had been designed to determine exactly that.

And she was sure of what she wanted. He had to give her some credit for that alone.

He took out a pad of paper and scrawled a rough draft of his verdict for the clinic administrator. He made a note for his secretary to type it up and copy it to Tabitha Monroe. Then he slipped it into the folder marked Tourbier, Melanie, J. closed it and set it aside.

It was time to move on.

Ten

"You've changed your mind?" Jeff's voice was incredulous. "Glory be, what happened? Did you get hit over the head with a ton of bricks?"

"In a manner of speaking, yes." Melanie leaned back on her bed and stared at the ceiling. It was three in the morning, Texas time, and she didn't feel close to falling asleep. Fortunately, it was already a civilized time of day in Britain and Jeff had been at his desk when she called. "I really got to thinking about what I was undertaking and I decided that if God, or whoever," she added in deference to Jeff's atheism, "had wanted me to have a child, he wouldn't have made it so hard for me to get pregnant."

"That's just bad luck, sweetie," Jeff said, unwilling, as always, to believe in any kind of fate. "When you meet the right man and start having the kind of physical relationship that goes along with that, you'll be popping kids out like Pez, just wait and see."

Melanie laughed and rolled over on her side. "Oh, Jeff, you have such a way of putting things."

"So what about this Jared Cross fellow?" Jeff asked. "Think he's a good prospect for a Pez dispenser?"

...nie hadn't told Jeff about her night with Jared, ...urprised her that he would make such a sug-...on. "What on earth makes you ask a thing like ...?"

Jeff's gasp was audible over the line. "Melanie Fourbier, you've fallen in love with him, haven't you?"

"That's crazy!"

"Yes, it *is* crazy!" She could picture his thin arms flailing dramatically. "Why did you do that?"

"I'm *not* in love with Jared Cross," Melanie said forcefully. "He's my therapist and we've agreed that that's *all* he's going to be."

"Aha! So you've talked about it."

Melanie sighed. "Yes, we did. We had...feelings, but we agreed there was no point in indulging them. For one thing, if we did, then my case would be passed along to someone else who might not be open-minded to my particular circumstances."

"Which wouldn't matter now, since you've changed your mind."

"He made it clear he doesn't want a relationship, Jeff."

"He dumped you?"

"No, he didn't dump me. I wasn't his to dump. He just made it clear that he's not a relationship person and, to tell you the truth, I found it really refreshing to find that out right up front."

"Ah, I see. So what's actually happening here is

that you're running away from this as much as he is.''

"I'm not running away from anything," she said without much conviction. "Who wants to be involved with someone who doesn't want to be there?''

"Who says he doesn't want to be there?''

"He does.''

"And you believe that?''

"Yes, I do.''

Jeff gave a dramatic sigh. "Okay. If that's what you choose to believe. Personally I think it's because you don't want to risk having another man in your life, but whatever. It's okay with me if it means you'll be coming home sooner. When are you coming home anyway?''

She swallowed a lump in her throat. "As soon as possible. The sooner I put Mission Creek behind me, the better.''

She hung up the phone with Jeff and lay in the dark for perhaps half an hour, tossing and turning and trying to sleep. Her mind raced, thinking of Jared, and of the children in the day-care center, and of the baby she wanted so badly for herself. It really was the right decision, she told herself. If God had wanted her to have a baby, he wouldn't have made it so difficult. There had to be a reason it hadn't worked out that way for her. She had to believe that. Otherwise, it was all too heartbreaking.

At four in the morning, she gave up and turned on the light. She wasn't going to sleep, that much was clear. It was Saturday morning, so she didn't need to go anywhere anyway. If she got tired later, she'd try to take a nap.

She went into the gleaming white kitchen that The Aldon Towers had equipped not only with a coffee-maker but with a minibar stocked daily with freshly ground coffee. It was better than the stuff she was used to getting in London and she felt a pang of regret at leaving this coffee behind when she went.

Deep down, she realized that it wasn't really about the coffee, but it was easier to think it was than to admit that maybe her feelings for Jared Cross went deeper than mere interest and curiosity. Deeper than simple affection.

She loved him.

But he'd made his position clear; he didn't want a relationship. If there was one thing she knew about Jared, it was that he was the most stubborn, willful, bullheaded man she'd ever met. Once he made up his mind about something, there was no changing it.

She put the coffee on to brew and took out the Yellow Pages and the telephone. She looked up airlines, then started to dial the number of the airline she'd flown in on from Dallas. But no sooner had she dialed the last digit than a picture she'd pegged to the refrigerator caught her eye. The picture Peter Wickham had drawn of her, Jared and a baby. Tears filled her eyes and spilled down her cheeks. She didn't want to leave yet. She didn't want to just hop on a plane and leave all those children she'd grown so fond of.

And in a strange way, she felt that if she left now, she would be leaving the dream of her own child forever.

She couldn't leave yet, she decided. She'd stay one more week. That would give Em time to find someone else to help out, if she wanted to, and it would give Melanie time to get herself together and not feel as if she was running away. She'd run enough in her lifetime. It was time to slow down.

It was time to grow up.

Next week at the day-care center, Melanie found herself repeatedly looking for Jared. He didn't seem to come around nearly as much as he had before and, once or twice when they did run into each other, he was cordial but distant. Decidedly distant.

Melanie might have thought she was being hypersensitive if Em hadn't noticed and commented on it herself.

"Melanie, dear, forgive me for prying, but did you and Dr. Cross have a falling-out?"

Melanie's face must have registered pain, because Em immediately said, "I shouldn't have asked. Please forgive me, I'm always sticking my nose in where it doesn't belong. It's just that I care about the two of you."

"It's okay, Em. I appreciate that. And to answer your question, no, we didn't have a falling-out." Which was true. There hadn't been an argument or a misunderstanding. They were just going their separate ways. It happened to people all the time. "I think Jared has a very heavy caseload right now."

"Mmm." Em nodded but looked as if she didn't believe it. "And are you doing okay?"

"I'm fine," she assured the older woman. "But there is something I need to speak with you about. I'm going back to London next week."

Now it was Em's turn to look sad. "No, really? For good?"

Melanie nodded.

"When do you plan to leave?"

"I'm thinking Thursday."

Em looked concerned. "Is there any way you might make it the following week?"

Melanie didn't particularly want to put off her departure any longer than necessary, but Em looked so serious that she said, "I can if you need me to stick around."

"I really could use you," Em said, with an apologetic look. "I have a few appointments that I'd rather not have to reschedule."

"Is everything all right?" Melanie asked, instantly alarmed.

Em let out a small sigh. "I had an iffy mammogram and the doctor wants to go in and do a biopsy. I've been down this road before and it's always fine, knock wood, but my mother had breast cancer and I'm a higher risk than most."

"Oh, Em. Of course I'll wait until that's over. My gosh, I'd want to stick around and make sure you were all right even if you didn't need me to help with the kids.'' She laid a hand on Em's arm. ''Thank you for confiding in me.''

''Thank *you* for your concern.'' Em smiled. ''Though I have to say, I'm still so darn sorry you're leaving. I was counting on having you around for months.'' She lowered her voice. ''I was hoping you'd have the baby here.''

''Actually, there isn't going to be a baby.''

Em put a hand to her lips. ''My goodness, I could have sworn... I'm so sorry, my dear. So sorry.''

''It's okay. It's a decision I made myself.''

''So Dr. Cross wasn't the problem?''

''No, as a matter of fact, Dr. Cross made me see the answer. I'm going to thank him this afternoon.''

''He is a wise man. But you were so looking forward to— Well, I just hope you know what you're doing.''

''Please don't worry about me, Em, especially with all you've got going on. I'm truly fine. This is for the best.''

Em gave a kind smile. ''You will keep in touch once you're back in England, won't you?''

''Of course I will. In fact, I was thinking I'd give you a digital camera so you can take pictures of the kids and keep me up-to-date on their progress. Would you mind?''

''Heavens, no, it would be a delight. As long as I can figure out how to work the thing.''

"It's easy," Melanie assured her. "I'll give you a quick lesson before I leave."

The door to the nursery opened and Melanie reflexively jerked her head toward it. When she saw Jared's secretary, Wendy, her heart sank but immediately her curiosity was piqued.

"Miss Tourbier," Wendy said, picking her way across the toy-strewn floor. "Dr. Cross sent me."

"Excuse me," Em said tactfully. "I see there's a finger-paint situation developing over there." She gave Melanie's shoulder a warm pat. "We'll talk more later."

Melanie nodded, then turned back to Wendy. "Dr. Cross sent you to see me?"

"Yes, he wanted me to tell you that your appointment this week has been canceled."

"Canceled? Did he reschedule?"

Wendy shrugged. "I don't think so. He just told me to tell you that the two of you weren't meeting anymore. He said you'd understand."

Well, she didn't. Was this his way of completely dismissing her? She had planned to tell him of her own change of plans in their meeting, but she hadn't told him yet. Which meant he still thought she was eager for the fertility treatments. Which meant he was just blowing her off right in the middle of her treatment with him, without regard to her feelings or plans. And he was even doing it through a third party, too cowardly to tell her himself how he was letting her down.

Which meant he was exactly like all the other men she'd ever gotten involved with.

Her blood boiled. "Is Dr. Cross alone in his office right now?" she asked Wendy, trying to maintain control.

Wendy must have sensed her ire, though. "Er, he is, but I don't think he wants to be interrupted."

"Well, I don't care if he wants to be or not, he's going to be." She was angrier than she'd ever been in her life. "Em!" she called across the room.

Em raised her head.

Melanie pointed upward. "I have to speak with someone. I'll be back in a few minutes, okay?"

"Take your time." Em nodded sagely. "We'll be fine."

"Ooh, Miss Tourbier, I really don't think this is a good idea," Wendy began. "Dr. Cross has not been in a great mood lately and—"

"I'll tell him you tried to stop me, Wendy."

She looked relieved. "Thanks."

Melanie hurried through the corridors to the elevators feeling angrier than she'd ever been in her life. How dare he? she wondered, pushing the elevator button and standing back to wait. How dare he make love to her and then drop her, both personally and professionally?

She couldn't recall ever feeling so betrayed.

The worst part was that she had really come to care about Jared. She'd even toyed with the idea of sticking around Mission Creek on a semipermanent basis. There was nothing in London to call her back, apart from the distance it would now put between her and Jared Cross.

She pressed the elevator button again, then again.

Finally the doors opened and she stepped into the car, remembering her first meeting with Jared on an elevator. She'd found him attractive right from the beginning. Somehow her instincts, which were normally pretty good even though she tended to ignore them, had failed to warn her that this guy might be trouble.

Well, that wouldn't matter from now on. From now on, she was going to use her head, not her heart— and her head knew beyond all shadow of a doubt that she was avoiding romantic relationships. Period.

Especially with someone like Jared Cross.

She didn't bother to knock. She simply pushed the door open and asked, "Who do you think you are?"

Jared looked up from his papers, surprised. For a moment she thought she even saw pleasure in his eyes. "Melanie—"

"Were you even going to tell me?"

"Tell you what? What are you talking about?"

"I'm talking about Wendy's message," she said, trying to hold back the tears that suddenly pricked her eyes. "You're not meeting with me anymore? Just like that? And you don't even have the courtesy to tell me yourself?''

''Melanie, you've mis—''

''After all we've been through together? After we…'' She swallowed a lump of emotion. ''I should have had you removed from the case when I first wanted to. At least then we never would have—''

''Slow down, Melanie—''

''I've met some pretty low-down guys in my lifetime,'' she said, pacing in front of his desk. ''But, then, you know that, don't you? You're the one who forced me to open up and talk about the most private parts of my life. And why? So you could dump me like last week's trash?''

''That's enough!'' he barked. ''If you'd just shut your mouth for a minute and listen—''

''Listen? Why? So you can feed me a bunch of lies? Tell me that this has nothing to do with our sleeping together, that it's strictly professional?''

''It is.'' He stood up and came around the desk. ''Isn't that how you wanted it?''

''Oh, I wanted it professional, all right,'' she said. ''But *this* is not professional.''

''Melanie, stop.''

''No.'' She whirled to face him. ''I'm not taking this kind of treatment anymore, do you understand me? I won't stand for it.'' She shook her head angrily. ''I didn't expect this of you, Jared, I really didn't. But

I guess I should have. You're just like the rest of them.''

"The rest of who?"

"Men! You're all alike."

He caught her by the arm and pulled her roughly toward him. "You don't know what you're talking about."

"Yes, I do." She tried to wrench her arm free. "For the first time I'm *very* clear on what's going on here."

They stood for a moment, nose to nose, glaring at each other heatedly.

"You are the most impossible woman I've ever met in my life."

"From you, that's a compliment."

"I didn't betray you."

She gave a spike of humorless laughter. "What would you call it, then?"

A muscle twitched in his jaw as he stared down at her.

Chills crossed over her body. His green eyes looked into hers as if they were looking straight to the bottom of her soul. Despite her anger, despite her mistrust, despite all of her pain, her heart leaped in response to his gaze and her body tingled at the proximity of his beautiful, sculpted mouth to hers.

She tilted her face up toward his, wishing with all her might that he'd kiss her and make this unpleasantness go away.

He did kiss her. And for just a moment, it seemed that their problems did disappear. As his mouth moved over hers, she thought she felt in him the same hunger for her that she felt for him.

She felt light-headed as a tingle ran down her back and into her core. When Jared's tongue touched hers, it was as if someone had lit that tingle on fire. Her body's response was immediate and desperate. She clutched at his back, pressing her hands against the lean, muscled physique that she already knew by heart.

He traced his hands down her back, then cupped them at her bottom, pulling her hips toward him. Toward his hips. She could tell he wanted her as much as she wanted him.

If only they could forget about the things that separated them. If only they were without issues and baggage to keep them apart.

If only they were two different people.

Jared drew back first and looked down at Melanie with fire in his eyes.

"You're right," he said, his breath hot against her mouth. "I haven't been professional enough."

"No kidding," she retorted, straightening her back and trying to keep her knees from feeling so weak.

"If I'd been truly professional I would have passed your case along from the beginning."

It all came back to her. The anger, the hurt, the betrayal. The confusion. How could he have just dumped her that way? And how could she bring herself to kiss him and want him so desperately after he'd treated her that way?

"Passing the case along from the beginning beats the heck out of passing it along now," she said.

"I didn't pass it along."

She stepped back, stunned. "What?"

"I didn't pass it along. I closed the case."

Eleven

Melanie suddenly felt weak. He hadn't passed her case to someone else, he'd dismissed it out of hand. That was worse. She wouldn't have thought he was capable of such patently cruel treatment.

The room spun. She groped for the back of the chair and sat down, ashamed of her weakness even as she succumbed to it.

"Melanie." Jared's strong arms guided her into the chair. "Are you all right? Can you hear me?"

She nodded, numb. What was going on? She thought she was going to pass out. "I heard you."

"You've gone as white as a sheet. What's the matter?"

She focused on his face, which seemed full of concern, and felt her heart sink. "Nothing, I skipped breakfast. I'm sure it's just low blood sugar." She wasn't about to admit how hurt she felt because of what he'd done.

"That doesn't sound like you," he said. "Maybe you should get checked out, make sure it's nothing serious."

"How do you know if it's like me or not?" she

returned, feeling better now that she was sitting down. "You don't even know me."

Something in his eyes retreated. "Maybe I don't."

"You've picked a fine time to admit that, now that you've rejected my application."

"Rejected your application?" He frowned. "What are you talking about? I approved it."

"I'm talking about you—" She stopped as she rewound her mental tape of what he'd just said. "You approved it?"

"Yes," he said, stepping back and looking at her with more anger than concern. "That's why I told Wendy to tell you to set up an appointment with the clinic administrator. So you could decide how and when to proceed with your treatment."

Melanie closed her eyes for a moment and tried to breathe. "Wendy didn't mention that part."

"Did you give her a chance?"

"Yes…" She thought about it. "Maybe."

He leaned against the desk and crossed his arms in front of him. "You were so ready to fly off the handle at me that you didn't even bother to get the facts first."

Her face grew warm. "I wouldn't have made this mistake if you had spoken to me personally."

"I have a full schedule," he said, without meeting her eyes.

"Full schedule, huh?" She opened her arms and made a point of looking around the room. "Looks like you're free right now."

"I'm not. In fact, when you burst in here, I was in the process of putting together a report on a patient who's about to be hospitalized."

She hesitated, unsure whether she believed him. "You still could have told me yourself."

His voice softened fractionally. "I thought we agreed it was best if we didn't see each other anymore."

"But for something like this—"

"*Especially* for something like this." He expelled a long breath. "This is about you moving on, starting that family you want, and then going back to London to live. It has nothing to do with me."

"Do you always send Wendy to give your patients a verdict?"

"No," he admitted. "I usually just have Wendy call. If she gets an answering machine, she leaves a message. See, usually, people are so happy about this news that they don't care how it's delivered. Why aren't you happy?"

She bit down on her lower lip to keep it from trembling. Why was she suddenly so emotional? And why couldn't she keep control of those emotions at least long enough to talk to Jared coherently and then leave his office? She swallowed, hard. "Because I've changed my mind. I'm not going to go forward with the treatment."

"Excuse me?"

"I'm not going to have fertility treatments." She didn't meet his eyes. "I'm giving up."

"On using the Mission Creek Clinic or on the idea of having a baby altogether?"

"The whole enchilada," she answered with a quick shake of the head. "No baby."

He gave nothing away with his eyes. "What changed your mind?"

She shrugged. "I guess I decided that if I was meant to have a baby, it wouldn't take so much work."

"I see." He stood up and walked slowly around his desk to his chair. "What made you decide that?"

"You did, actually."

"I did?"

She nodded. "In our last session you said a few things that hadn't really occurred to me before. At least not in the way you presented them." She gave a weak shrug. "Anyway, I figure if I was meant to have a baby, I would have gotten pregnant without all this work."

He looked hesitant. "Not that I disagree with your decision, but I'm not sure I'd put a lot of stock in fate."

She smiled. "That's one more big difference between you and me."

"And so you're leaving?" he asked, sitting down.

She nodded. "The week after next. Em wanted me to stay on and help a little longer or I'd already be gone."

His jaw tightened along with his tone. "It's very nice of you to stay and help Em."

"It's the least I could do. She's been so kind to me." Her voice was stilted, as if she were talking to a complete stranger and not a man she'd made passionate love to just a week ago.

"Well." He placed his hands, palms down, on the desk and gave Melanie a blank look, as if he didn't know what to do with himself. "I guess that's that. I'll let the clinic know."

"Thanks." She was reluctant to leave, because it seemed there was still so much left unresolved. But what could she say? What could either one of them say to resolve it? There was nothing. She stood before him and extended her hand. "Thanks, Jared, for taking the time to consider my case."

For a moment, he sat still. Then, reluctantly, he took her hand, and his touch sent shivers up her arm. "Just doing my job," he said, holding her captive with his eyes.

She looked away. "I guess I'll see you around."

"I'm not so sure about that. I don't get to London that often and you...well, I guess you won't be coming back to Mission Creek."

"Not unless fate brings me here."

"Then that's that."

She drew her hand back and suddenly felt very cold and very alone. "Yes, that's that. Goodbye, Jared," she said, trying to keep the waver of emotion from her voice. "Goodbye."

The next week passed very slowly for Melanie. She already felt she had jet lag, in anticipation of her trip home. It was as if once she'd decided she was leaving, her mind was gone. She was tired all the time, it was hard to concentrate on what she was doing, and she wanted nothing more than to get on that plane and get as far away from Jared Cross as she could.

Because every minute she spent in Mission Creek now, she spent wondering if she was going to run into him. She looked for him down every corridor she walked in the hospital, on every crowded elevator, and each time the day-care door opened, her heart skipped a beat.

But it was never him.

Once she saw him going into the cafeteria while she was walking one of the children to the third-floor nurses' station, where his mother was waiting. For a moment Melanie stood frozen between impulses to run toward Jared and to run in the opposite direction. If she had not been holding the hand of the child, she might have done one or the other. Instead, she kept steady on her course and hoped he didn't see her.

He didn't.

As the end of her time in Mission Creek neared, Melanie made one final appointment with Tabitha Monroe. She wanted to say goodbye, but she also wanted to talk to Tabitha about making a financial donation for the day-care center to purchase more games and computers for the kids.

"Melanie, you've already been so generous with the maternity wing and the nursery," Tabitha said when Melanie told her what she had in mind. "Not to mention all the time you've donated to the day-care center. I feel like we've taken advantage of you."

"No, I want to help," Melanie insisted. "This place, and more to the point, the people here, have come to mean a great deal to me. More than I can say. If there's anything I can do to make things easier for them, or more fun for the kids, I truly want to do it."

Tabitha gave her a brilliant smile. "You're really something else, you know that? We're so lucky you came to Mission Creek."

"No, I'm the lucky one," Melanie said, but her voice was tinged with sadness. She was glad she'd come, because she'd made some wonderful friends and, more to the point, she'd had a tremendously important revelation about her life and the direction she was going to take. Or at least the direction she *wasn't* going to take.

But that was the problem. It was hard to leave her dreams of playgrounds and cookouts and PTA meetings behind.

Just thinking about it made her eyes burn with tears, so she changed the subject. "I'd like to give you a check made out to the hospital, if that's all right with you."

"Absolutely."

Melanie reached down to the ground for her purse, but suddenly she felt woozy and weak.

"Melanie?" Tabitha's voice was sharp, alert. She was at Melanie's side in an instant. "You okay, honey?"

"Fine," Melanie said. "Just a little tired. I don't suppose you have any coffee around here, do you?"

"Sure do. Right outside, I'll get you some." She got up and started for the door, then stopped and turned back. "Decaf?"

Melanie shook her cloudy head. "High-test. Black. I need the energy. I've just been exhausted lately."

With a curious look, Tabitha went out the door and returned a couple minutes later with two steaming ceramic mugs. She set one on a coaster on the desk in front of Melanie. "There you go. It's hot, be careful."

"Thanks." Melanie took the mug and raised it to her lips. But before it ever got there, the smell touched her nose and she felt a wave of nausea. "Oh," she said, letting out a long breath. "I am really not well."

Tabitha was quick to remove the coffee cup and replace it with water from a clear glass pitcher on her desk. "Try this."

Melanie took a sip of the cold water. It made her feel a little better. "I'm sorry," she said, when she'd collected herself. "I don't know what's the matter with me. Maybe I'm getting the flu. We all know I'm not pregnant, after all."

"Are you sure?" Tabitha asked.

"Pretty sure. I've decided against going through with the procedure."

"Do you mind if I ask you why you changed your mind?"

Melanie explained how she'd changed her mind and her theory that if she was meant to have a baby, she wouldn't have had so much trouble conceiving.

Tabitha listened in silence, nodding now and then as if she really understood what Melanie was feeling.

Tabitha leaned back in her chair. "I have a lot of faith in fate, believe me, but every once in a while, I think it can use a little push."

"Well, it had a big push a few years ago, and nothing happened."

"It must have been very hard. I hope I'm not making you feel uncomfortable by bringing all this up."

"Of course not." Melanie waved the notion away. "Not at all. Look, two weeks ago, I would have been thrilled at the prospect." She gave a wistful smile. "But that was before…" She was about to say "before Jared talked me out of it" when she remembered the day that had happened. More specifically, the *night* that had happened. "Do you have a calendar?" she asked suddenly.

Bemused, Tabitha turned a small Buddha on her desk to face Melanie. There was a calendar set into his belly.

Melanie lifted the statue and, remembering something she'd heard in Japan many years ago about it being good luck to rub the Buddha's belly, gave it a quick rub then studied the small grid inside. It had been two weeks since she and Jared had made love.

Was it possible she was *pregnant?*

Hope surged in her, but she dismissed the idea quickly. "No way," she said, setting the Buddha back down on the desk.

"No way what?" Tabitha asked, raising an eyebrow.

"Nothing, it's too absurd to even say."

"Melanie, you know I'm your friend, right?"

Melanie smiled. "I certainly feel that you are."

"And you know you can trust me?"

"Sure. But, really, there's nothing to it. I thought..." She hesitated, then let out a sigh. "For one stupid moment there I guess I hoped I might be pregnant but I'm not."

"Is it possible?"

"No way," Melanie said vehemently.

"'No way' because you don't believe it or 'no way' because it would have to be a miracle?"

Melanie nodded. "I have a physical problem that makes it almost impossible for me to get pregnant. It's like a one-in-a-million shot. Even with fertility treatments, it's very unlikely. And I didn't have the treatments."

"But did you have sex?" Tabitha asked bluntly.

Melanie pressed her lips together, considered the woman before her and decided she could trust her. She nodded slowly. "Once."

"About—" Tabitha glanced at the Buddha's belly "—oh, say, a couple of weeks ago?"

"Yes," Melanie admitted. Tabitha was wrong. She

knew there was no way she'd gotten pregnant after her one night with Jared. She wasn't some young, fertile teenager who was unrealistic about getting pregnant the first time or something. She was a grown woman. And Jared was a grown man. Together they had taken the precaution that any responsible adult does in this day and age, although they had been a little late in slipping it on....

"I'm getting you a pregnancy test," Tabitha said, and stood up.

"Wait a minute," Melanie said. "That's not necessary."

"Can't hurt." Tabitha's eyes twinkled. "Call me crazy, but I think maybe fate has made an appearance in your life after all."

Twelve

Melanie held the stick with a trembling hand and watched the liquid cross the test window. A moment later one faint pink line appeared on the pregnancy test. One line, not two. The test line.

Not pregnant.

With a familiar feeling of hopelessness, she tossed the stick into the trash can and threw herself into the club chair that looked perfectly logical in the luxurious bathroom of The Aldon Towers.

That luxury wasn't doing her a whole lot of good right now. The gilded mirrors, Italian marble tile, silk sheets and every other luxury her money could afford did nothing to quell the loneliness that raged in her so strongly she almost feared it would stop her heart.

She wasn't pregnant. So what was the surprise? She hadn't been pregnant for years now. This was probably the thousandth stick she'd peed on and she'd never seen more than one line. Even after trying so hard when she was married. Why did she presume to hope she was pregnant now, when she'd had sex just once in the past few years, and they'd used a condom? It was foolish of her to even hope.

And it was even more foolish of her to cry about

it now, but she did cry. She couldn't stop herself. Her heart was breaking. She cried for the children she had imagined all her life but whom she'd never meet and never get to love. She cried for the parents she had lost. She cried for the child she'd been when she had suddenly found herself alone, and she cried for the love she'd always imagined was waiting for her somewhere in the world that would ease that loss.

And she cried for Jared.

As crazy as she knew it was, she felt he was the one for her and she'd lost her chance with him. She missed him. She longed for him as if she'd loved him all her life.

Sobs racked her body until her stomach and head ached and she knew she was going to be sick.

She went to the sink and poured a cup of cool water, but this time it didn't make her feel better. This time her stomach lurched and she barely made it to the toilet on time.

Afterward she leaned her head against the cool marble wall and thought she'd never felt so alone in her life.

But she'd had it with feeling sorry for herself. She had to find some purpose, take her life by the reins again and steer it someplace useful. Determined, though still wobbly, she put her hands on the toilet seat and started to hoist herself up when she noticed the stick in the bottom of the fancy gold wastebasket. It had been sitting for perhaps five minutes, maybe a little more, but it never would have occurred to her to look at it if she hadn't been down on the floor anyway. But there it was, and she could see it as clear as day.

There were two pink lines on it.

Jared looked at the two pieces of yellow paper that Wendy had left on his desk. "While you were out..." they each said, then Wendy had jotted Melanie's name at two different times. Melanie hadn't left a message, other than that she'd called. He didn't even know where she was so he could call her back.

Not that it would be very hard to find her. If she wasn't at home, she was probably working at the hospital. Otherwise, she'd be somewhere in between the two and a message at one would get to her eventually.

The truth was, he didn't want to call. He didn't want to hear her voice and feel the ache he felt every time he thought of her. He didn't want to remember what it felt like to run his hands over her soft form. He didn't want to start questioning his decision to stop seeing her. Because, really, there was nothing to question. She was going back to London, and there was no way they could carry on a long-distance relationship. And there would be no point in doing it, even if they decided to try.

Logic gave him all the answers he needed. The problem was that his heart—or some other equally illogical organ—kept giving him bad information.

There was a knock at his door and he looked up as Tabitha Monroe entered.

"Hi, Jared," she said, smiling that knockout smile of hers. "Got a minute to chat?"

"Sure, Tabitha." Anything to keep his mind off Melanie. "What's on your mind?"

"Melanie Tourbier."

He groaned inwardly. "What about her?"

"Well, I'll be honest with you, Jared. I'm here as a friend, not so much in a professional capacity."

"Okay." He frowned. "Please, have a seat and tell me what this is all about."

She sat and crossed her legs. "Melanie told me once that the two of you had some real knock-down-drag-out fights during the time you were counseling her."

"I'm not sure I'd characterize them that way, but we did have some friction at times."

She gave a wan smile. "What interested me was the fact that you had any conflict at all. That's not like you."

He tapped his fingers on the desk. "Melanie Tourbier brings out the worst in me I guess."

"I think she brings *something* out in you." Tabitha looked at him directly. "But I don't think it's the worst."

Tabitha had known Jared for a long time. In fact, she knew too much about him. He hated that.

"What are you getting at, Tabitha?" he asked, even though he didn't really want to hear the answer.

"Jared Cross, you know darn well what I'm getting

at. Now, I've never interfered in your private life before, but this time I have to say something. I think you're in love with Melanie Tourbier and if you let her go back to London, it's going to be a huge mistake.''

Jared's mouth dropped open. "In love with Melanie Tourbier?" he repeated incredulously. "Because I didn't get along with her?"

Tabitha lowered her chin and looked up at him through narrowed eyes. "I think you didn't get along with her because you're in love with her."

He gave an unconvincing laugh. "Who's the psychiatrist here?"

"Physician heal thyself." She raised an eyebrow. "Stop that woman from leaving."

"I can't stop her from leaving, she's going home. She doesn't live here. She doesn't even live on this continent."

"I don't think anyplace feels like home to her," Tabitha said calmly. "I think she's still looking. Mission Creek might be just the place for her."

He knew better. A woman like Melanie, who had traveled the globe many times over and dined with kings and queens could never be happy in a tiny Texas town like Mission Creek. "Sorry, Tabitha, but you've got the wrong idea about Melanie and me."

"I'm sorry to hear it," she said, sighing. "But I do hope you'll keep what I said in mind. Melanie's a very special woman. She's one in a million. It would be a real shame to let her go.''

He knew it.

But he had no choice.

Melanie reported for her last day at the day-care center with a heavy heart. She was really going to miss it here. It was hard to believe she'd only been in Mission Creek for a few short weeks, because somehow it felt like home. London seemed a very long way away, and not just in distance. It was a long way away emotionally, too.

Part of her wanted to stay in Mission Creek, to make it her home. But that would be very difficult, considering the fact that she was carrying Jared Cross's baby and he wasn't even returning her calls. He was making it painfully clear that he wanted nothing more to do with her—in fact, he'd said as much at their last meeting—so that was that. She didn't need to stick around and let him reject her *and* their baby.

Not that she could really imagine him rejecting a child....

''Melanie?'' It was Em, coming in from her doctor's appointment. ''How did everything go without me this morning?''

''Oh, fine,'' Melanie said, ''though the kids missed you. The important thing is you. How are you doing?''

Em beamed. ''Just fine. They went in to do a biopsy but it was just a cyst. They aspirated it and let me go.''

Melanie felt a huge rush of relief. "I'm so glad to hear it, Em."

"You and me both."

"And that's it? You don't need to follow up?"

"Just my usual checkups."

"Great news. But do you really feel well enough to come in and work today? Because I don't mind covering for you. Maybe you should go home and get some rest."

"No need. Not only did they not do the procedure, but I actually got to sleep a little late this morning because of my appointment. Now I'm ready and raring to go."

Melanie didn't say it, but she was glad Em had some energy, because Melanie was exhausted. She knew the pregnancy had something to do with it, but she suspected it had more to do with Jared. She wanted to see him so badly, yet she knew she was being a fool for another man who wasn't right for her. This internal war she was having was wearing her out.

The sooner she got out of Texas, the better. Her life was changing now, her priorities were changing. She was going to be a mother, so it was time she started thinking like one instead of like a heartsick schoolgirl.

The day passed surprisingly fast as Melanie tried to savor every moment with the kids she'd come to adore. By five-thirty all the kids were gone and Melanie knew she had to say goodbye to Em.

"You're really part of the family, Melanie," Em said with tears in her eyes. She held Melanie's hands. "I don't know how we're going to get along without you!"

"Don't say that." Melanie smiled and sniffled. "This is hard enough already."

"Think you'll ever come back and visit us?" Em asked.

"I don't know." She thought of Jared and what it might be like to come visit in a year or two. Would he have met someone else? Maybe even married? She couldn't bear the thought. "We'll see," she said, then gave Em's hands a squeeze and let go.

A ruckus in the hallway caught their attention and they went to the door of the day-care center and looked out. The corridor was crowded with doctors, nurses and orderlies escorting about ten women patients, some with IVs on, away from the new wing.

"What's going on?" Em asked.

"All the power's gone out in the new wing," a nurse answered. "We're moving the patients to the third and fourth floors."

"Can we help?" Melanie asked.

"We'd sure appreciate it," the nurse answered. "They're setting up a makeshift nursery on the third floor. I think they've already moved the infants there, but you can go check with Dr. Delaney. He's overseeing the move."

"We're on our way," Em said, and she and Melanie made their way into the dimly lit maternity wing.

"Isn't there an emergency generator?" Melanie asked, looking around at the disconcertingly dark halls.

"There should be." Em looked concerned. "This is mighty strange."

A tremor passed through Melanie's chest, but she tried to ignore it. This was no time to panic.

"Ah, there's Dr. Delaney," Em said, approaching a distinguished-looking gentleman with white hair and a white mustache. "Have all the patients been moved, Doctor?" she asked.

"They have. Everyone's safe and sound."

"That's good news."

Melanie looked for relief but felt none. "Is there anything we can do to help, Doctor?"

"As a matter of fact, there is. Em, you remember Moira Burns, don't you?"

"Yes, of course. She used to work in the cafeteria."

"Right. Well, Moira's in a real tizzy about the power outage. She's sure it means something terrible's going to happen." Dr. Delaney shrugged. "I tried to calm her down, but she'd hear none of it. She always liked you. Maybe you could succeed where I failed."

"I'd be glad to try," Em said.

"Thank you. She's been moved to Room 315." Dr. Delaney turned his attention to Melanie. "Now, if you wouldn't mind going to the storage room down the hall on the left and picking up some blankets, that would be a big help.''

"I'd be glad to," Melanie said.

"It's right there." Dr. Delaney pointed along the corridor. "Around the corner to the left. A nurse, Caitlyn Matthews, is there collecting things. Just ask her what to bring."

"Will do." Melanie started down the hall, glad for something to do to help. She wasn't ready to leave the hospital for the last time yet.

She followed Dr. Delaney's instructions and ended up in another corridor with several other people.

A small blond woman, with very short hair and tons of energy, was handing out supplies to people and issuing orders.

"Caitlyn Matthews?" Melanie guessed.

"That's right," the woman answered, dragging her forearm across her forehead. "Whew! It's getting hot in here. Who are you?"

"Melanie Tourbier." She smiled. "Dr. Delaney told me to ask you what I can do to help."

"Another pair of arms! Perfect!" Caitlyn smiled broadly. "Let's see. Dr. Walters was just saying we needed to take some more bottles—"

She was interrupted by a woman's scream.

Melanie's head jerked toward the sound just as a scrawny man with dirty-blond hair and a scruffy goatee raised a gun in the air and shot the ceiling. Plaster spilled down onto the gleaming white floor.

"That's the only warning you folks get," the man

said in a thin Texas twang. "No funny business, got it?"

"Who is that?" Melanie whispered. "What's going on?"

"It's Branson Hines," Caitlyn said under her breath. "And I don't know what's going on, but it isn't good."

Branson Hines! Melanie's stomach lurched into her throat. Branson Hines was a dangerous criminal who had no regard for life. She looked around. There were about eleven other people, including Caitlyn, a tall, dark-haired doctor in a lab coat, several orderlies and a few other people in street clothes like Melanie.

"Get in the storage room," Branson Hines said, waving the gun. "In there! *Now!*"

"What is it you want, Hines?" the doctor asked in a smooth, easy voice that sounded so calm even Melanie felt soothed by it. "Why do you want everyone in the storage room?"

"Because it's easier to keep hostages when they're all together," Hines said with a sneer. "I'd hate to have to shoot someone who tried to run away. It gets so messy."

Melanie's stomach twisted.

"You don't need all these people as hostages," the doctor went on. "Why don't you just keep me and let the others go?"

Hines narrowed his eyes. "I know you. You're Walters, aren't you? You're the one who let my son die."

"Your baby was stillborn," Dr. Walters said, not without compassion. "No one could save him."

Hines snorted. "No one *did* save him, you mean. You all pretended to care, but I know better. You think my wife and me's trash. You didn't want to get your hands dirty with us. But you're going to make that up to me now. To me and Deena."

"How can we make it up to you?" Caitlyn asked, her voice betraying a hint of a tremor. "It was a terrible tragedy, but it's over and we can't undo it."

Branson Hines leveled an ugly gaze on her and answered, in a voice mocking her own, "That's why you're gonna give me another baby. To replace the one you killed."

"Give you another baby!" Caitlyn gasped.

"It's not going to happen," Dr. Walters said.

"It is, or I'm going to pick you all off one by one." He took a step toward the group. "Starting with, hmm..." He aimed the gun at them and moved it, left to right, stopping in front of Melanie. "Starting with this pretty lady here."

Thirteen

Melanie's breath caught in her throat. "You can't trade me for an innocent baby," she said, her voice and her resolve stronger than she'd expected. "Even if they agreed, I wouldn't let them."

"We'll see about that." Hines was close enough that she could smell his rank breath and the days of perspiration that had dried on his clothes. "Into the storage room. All of you." He shot again, this time putting a hole the size of a football in the wall about twenty yards away.

"Do what he says," Dr. Walters said, leading the way, followed by Caitlyn Matthews.

Reluctantly the group moved into the storage room.

"Very good," Branson Hines said, leaning casually against the door frame and making a point of examining his gun before looking up at them. "Now, here's the deal." He shrugged a small backpack off his shoulder. "One of you is going to get on the phone and call the nursery. I want a baby boy with blond hair, and I want him here within five minutes. Otherwise—" he tapped the backpack "—there's a nice little bomb in here that will blow you all, and this whole damn wing, to smithereens."

Melanie tried to swallow, but her throat was as dry as cotton. She believed him. But there was no way on earth she would ever be a party to them giving this maniac a baby, nor could she picture anyone else in this room doing that—which meant there was a good possibility they were all going to die.

And she would never see Jared again. Never get the chance to tell him that she loved him. Never get the chance to tell him about their baby.

She'd never get the chance to hold their baby in her arms.

Tears burned at her eyes, but she refused to cry. She wasn't going to give this man the satisfaction of breaking her down. She was going to keep her hope up until the end. She had to do it, not only for her own sake, but for the baby, as well.

"Security is already on the way here," Caitlyn told Branson Hines. "There's absolutely no way you can get away with this. You must see that. But if you put the gun down now, you'd get a lighter sentence than you would if you harmed anyone."

For a moment, Hines looked uncertain. "Who sent for security?" he asked suspiciously.

"They were called when the lights went out," Dr. Walters said, anger tinging his voice. "We're not fools here, Hines. We knew something was wrong when the power went out and the emergency generator didn't kick in. Especially after that little stunt you pulled with the explosion outside the nursery."

"Some of my better work," Hines said with an evil

smile. "That was a warning. This is the real thing."
He pushed off the door frame and leveled the gun at
them again. "You," he said, pointing to Caitlyn with
the gun. "You've got a big mouth. You go over to
that phone and call whoever you have to to get that
baby here. Tell them the first hostage will be killed
in one half hour."

Caitlyn exchanged glances with Dr. Walters and
went to the telephone while Branson Hines covered
her with the gun.

She was only gone for a few minutes. When she
came back, she shrugged. "It's like I said. They're
not going to do it."

"Oh, they'll do it." Hines smiled again, revealing
teeth stained brown by nicotine. "They don't want all
that blood on this fancy new floor. Now I'm going to
close you all in here and I'm going to set this bomb
up out here. Touch the door and *boom!*" He fluttered
his arms. "You're all flying with the birds."

"Where are you going?" someone asked.

"I'm going to take care of security." His voice was
positively menacing. With one final hostile look, he
slammed the door shut and they all waited in silence
as he rattled away, presumably rigging the bomb outside the door.

No one spoke for several minutes after he left, then,
finally, Caitlyn broke the silence. "Should we try the
door?"

"No," Dr. Walters answered sharply. "We can't
take the chance."

"There must be another way out of here," Melanie said, looking around for a heating duct or loose panel in the ceiling. The room was so crowded with shelves, there wasn't a bare spot on the wall.

"I say we just wait until he comes back and then jump him," a small, bald orderly said. "He can't overpower us all."

"No, but he could shoot one of us," a nurse said. "And I don't think any of us wants to take the chance."

"No way," several people concurred.

"I'm never going to see my children again," one of the nurses cried, and began sobbing.

Melanie's heart constricted and she tried not to think about how her own parents must have felt if they knew, in those last few seconds before the explosion, that they were never going to see her again.

Melanie made her way over to the nurse and put a hand on the woman's shaking shoulders. "Yes, you are. You're going to see them tonight."

"I don't think so...." The woman's sobs intensified.

"We have to stay calm," Melanie said, feeling, for the first time since the ordeal had begun, that everything was going to be all right. She didn't know how, but she felt certain of it. "The security at the hospital is good. I'll bet they've already apprehended Branson Hines and are on their way over to rescue us right now."

"Do you really think so?" the nurse asked doubtfully.

"Well, I don't know, but I am sure that if it hasn't happened yet, it's about to. Branson Hines is no genius. This isn't a carefully laid out plan. It's the rash action of an angry man."

"That's true," the orderly who'd wanted to charge Hines said. "If he had a brain, he never would have thought it would work to ransom us for a baby. Why, I'll bet he's made mistakes left and right."

"That's right," Melanie agreed. "So all we have to do is relax as much as possible, conserve our energy and be ready to take action when and if the time comes." She sank down on the floor and leaned back against the shelf. A whirring sound caught her attention, then she heard a faint clanging sound behind her, as if someone was working in the distance.

She turned around to look for the source and noticed, behind two large boxes of bedpans, a wide air-conditioning vent!

Jared flipped the silver dollar for the twentieth time that day. Heads. Again. Which meant he should call Melanie and beg her to stay in Mission Creek.

How could it land on heads twenty times in a row?

Well, there was that one time it had landed on tails, but it had rolled off the desk and under the bookshelf, and he didn't think that counted. He had to be fair. Objective. This was science, after all.

Although there was something funny about it. The

same result twenty times in a row went against everything he'd learned in his high school and college math classes.

He dropped the coin into his pocket and picked up the telephone. He'd already dialed the first six digits of her phone number so many times he knew them by heart. This time he added the seventh and sat back while the telephone rang.

It rang and rang. Finally the line was picked up by the building's voice-mail system.

"Melanie," he said. "It's me. Jared. Jared Cross. Look, I know you're leaving tomorrow, but we need to talk. Anyway, I need to talk. I've been a real idiot and I know you probably don't want anything more to do with me. I can't really blame you, but..." He let out a breath he hadn't realized he was holding. "I'm a different man now. Or at least I'm trying to be. And it's thanks to you. You were right from the beginning—I wasn't being objective about your case. I think I've been too hard on a lot of cases. But you've made me realize that what matters most is a parent's love and devotion to a child, that anyone who's taking the trouble to come here and submit to our scrutiny is demonstrating a lot about their commitment right there. I guess I was so ticked off about my own experience that I couldn't see clearly...which is no excuse, but..." He was floundering. He sounded like an idiot. "Anyway, I was hoping you might forgive me and maybe we could get together and talk about us. And the future." No! He'd gone too far. He shouldn't have said that. He'd never played his hand so foolishly in his life. He had to stop the message before it went into the system for Melanie.

The pound key, something in his head said. That would delete the message. He pressed the pound key quickly and leaned back, letting out a long, relieved breath.

Until the recorded voice said, "Your message has been deposited."

Jared muttered an oath and slammed the phone down. Leave it to him to go blurting all that stuff on the only voice-mail system in the country that didn't give you options when you pushed the pound key.

Now what was he going to do?

He was going to face the music, that was what. Leave things up to the very fate Melanie thought had failed her. It wasn't as if he could go to her apartment and delete the message before she got it. Life was not a sitcom.

Jared was leaving his office for the evening, anticipating a long night of baseball and tortilla chips, and wondering if Melanie was going to call, when Em came scurrying up the hall toward him.

"Dr. Cross! Thank goodness you're still here. We need help."

The look on her face made his adrenaline surge. "What's wrong, Em?"

"Branson Hines," she sputtered. "He turned the power off in the maternity wing. We got the patients out, but he's taken hostages."

Jared went rigid. "Hostages?"

Em nodded and tears pooled in her eyes. "Including Melanie Tourbier."

"Where are they?" he asked, his voice deadly calm.

"In the storage room on the second floor, but no one can get in. Branson Hines has rigged it with a bomb." Her voice caught in a sob. "No one can get to them."

"I'll get to them," Jared said under his breath.

"Be careful!" Em called behind him as he hurried away. "No one knows where Branson is and he's got a gun."

If she said anything after that, he didn't hear it. All he could hear was the pounding of his own heart and the voice inside of him that said, *Get to her. Tell her you love her before it's too late.*

He thought he just might be able to do it, too. He knew the storage room Em meant. It was large, about four times the size of most of their storage closets. It had originally been built as an office, but they'd decided the space could better be used for storage.

It was a decision Jared would be grateful for forever, because, since it was originally going to be an office it had a good ventilation system. Specifically it had a large air-conditioning duct leading straight into it. He knew it well because one of his patients had taken to hiding there after her mother had given birth to a new baby. Eventually Jared had succeeded in helping the child accept her new sibling, but he'd never succeeded in getting the building maintenance staff to close off the duct.

Now he thanked God they hadn't closed it off.

Not wanting to wait for the elevator, Jared flew down the stairwells to the second floor, where a group of police officers had cordoned off the entry to the new wing.

Jared recognized one of them as the husband of one of the nurses who worked in pediatrics. "Tim," he said, approaching. "Where is Hines? Do they know?"

Tim shook his head. "We've got men checking out the security monitors, but unfortunately some of the monitors were knocked out along with the power. He could be anywhere."

Jared thought for a moment, wondering if he should tell Tim his plan. Part of him was reluctant, since he knew the police would try to talk him out of it. On the other hand, he was going to do it anyway, and he figured they should know in case something went wrong. Jared wasn't out to be a hero. He just wanted to get to Melanie.

He briefly told Tim about the duct and, as predicted, Tim tried to stop him.

"I've got to," Jared said firmly. "What's more, I'm probably the only one here who can do it without attracting Hines's attention, since he's almost certainly watching everyone in uniform."

Tim took off his hat and scratched his head.

"You're right about that. Tell you what, let me talk to the chief. You wait here."

Jared waited for a moment while Tim went to consult his chief, then he took off for the west hall, where the air-conditioning duct came out. He wasn't about to stand around and wait for the chief of police to tell him to go home and wait for a call when it was all over.

He slipped around the corner unnoticed and was glad to see the darkened hallway was empty. With a quick glance left and right he took a Swiss army knife out of his pocket and unscrewed the vent. Then he climbed in and pulled it shut behind him. It wasn't secure, but with any luck it would stay up and look like it was. He made his way through the cramped ductwork for several minutes, the thought of Melanie driving him forward. She was probably terrified. He remembered how she'd reacted when the bomb had gone off outside the nursery. She was probably a nervous wreck right now.

He couldn't wait to take her in his arms. He'd hold her all night. He'd hold her for a week, a month. Hell, he'd never let her go.

After a few minutes he got to the vent at the storage room. He heard her voice even before he saw her.

"There's a vent here," she was whispering. "If we can open it, maybe we can sneak out of here."

"Who knows where it leads?" someone asked. Jared thought it was the gloomy maintenance worker that everyone called "Eeyore." "What if we get stuck in it?"

"At least we won't be in *here*," Melanie responded with surprising spunk. "Wouldn't you rather be hidden in the duct than cowering under the nose of Branson Hines's gun?"

Jared smiled at the sound of her voice and moved right up next to the vent. "Melanie," he whispered.

She started. "Who said that?"

"In here." Jared tapped on the vent. "You're right, there's a vent, and you can all get out this way. Open it up."

"Jared?" she cried. "Is it really you?"

The others in the room spoke excitedly and came toward her.

"Yes, it's me." He smiled and put his hand to the vent.

She put hers against it. "I thought I'd never see you again."

"I couldn't let you go without taking you on the hospital duct tour," he said. "Now quick, open the vent and come through."

She pushed some boxes aside and said, "Help me move the shelves, you all. We might not have much time."

There was an excited murmur of voices as everyone stood and did as Melanie had instructed. Then Melanie went back to the vent and pulled.

"It's stuck," she said urgently. "We need a screwdriver."

"There's no screwdriver in here," Eeyore said.

"Here." Jared took the small Swiss army knife and shoved it through the slats, bending them as he forced it through.

"Got it." Melanie unscrewed the vent.

"Let me help with that," Sam Walters said, coming up to the vent. "Hey, Jared," he said, smiling.

"Long time," Jared said, smiling back. "Now get the damn vent off before Hines comes back."

Melanie and Sam pulled together and the vent came free.

As soon as he saw Melanie's face, Jared knew he was in love with her. And he knew he was never going to let her go, even if it meant he had to move to London and work at a gas station.

"My hero," Melanie said, her face glowing.

"Not if you don't get out of here," Jared said.

"Jared, you're going to have to lead the way," Sam said. "Go, quickly. Everyone stay calm, but keep moving." He helped Melanie into the duct and said, "Now go. I'll head up the rear. Come on, everyone."

One by one the hostages crawled into the duct and Jared led the way back to the hall. He had no way to tell how many people there were. All he knew was that Melanie was right behind him and she was going to be okay.

He was glad to see that the vent was still up when he got back to where he'd started. "This is it," he said, pushing the vent open. "Almost home free."

He got out and helped Melanie to her feet. He wanted nothing more than to take her in his arms, but there were other people to help first. Melanie stood by his side and helped him assist the others.

"There they are!" someone called, and three police officers came running toward them.

One of them was Tim. "You knew we'd tell you not to do it, didn't you?" he asked with a grin.

"I was pretty sure of it," Jared said.

Tim gave him a hearty pat on the back. "Well, all's well that ends well, as they say."

"Let's hope it ends well," Jared said grimly. "Have they got Hines yet?"

Tim's face grew serious. "No, not yet. But we know he's in here somewhere. There's no way he can get out of the building without getting caught."

"He's got a gun," Melanie said breathlessly. "And a backpack with a bomb in it."

"Would you mind giving the chief a full report?" Tim suggested. "I think they already have a pretty good idea of how he's armed and what he's up to, but you might be able to fill in some details."

"I'll go speak with him now," Melanie said.

Jared, meanwhile, was counting people as they came out. "How many of you were in there?" he asked Melanie.

"Twelve," she answered, looking over the group who had made it safely through the duct so far.

"Sam Walters isn't here yet. Who else?"

Melanie scanned the group. "Caitlyn," she quickly. "Caitlyn Matthews."

"Sam's nurse," Jared said. He poked his head the vent. "Sam?" he called. "Caitlyn?"

There was an answering silence.

"Where could they be?" Melanie asked fretfully. She'd been so sure they had all gotten out safely.

"Sam!" Jared called again. "Do you need me to come in?"

"Come on in," answered a voice. But it wasn't Sam's. "But make damn sure you bring that baby or your friends here are going to pay the price."

Jared knew exactly who was speaking, and it sent a chill right down his spine.

Branson Hines.

Fourteen

"Little change of plans," Branson said with a sneer at Caitlyn and Sam as he forced them through an opening he'd made into a conference room. "Looks like your pals jumped ship. You're not going to be so lucky. Come with me."

"What if we don't?" Sam asked.

Branson put the gun against Caitlyn's ribs. "Want the lady to get hurt?"

Sam met Caitlyn's eyes, tried to give a reassuring smile, then looked back at Hines. "Where do you want us to go?"

"Good thinking, Doc. There's a maintenance closet by the nurse's station. Lead the way. And don't forget if you make one false move, the lady gets it."

The gun was cold and hard against Caitlyn's ribs. Her instinct was to push it away, to stop the pressure, but she didn't dare.

They walked in silence down the hall and to the maintenance closet.

"Open the door," Hines instructed.

Sam opened the door and turned on the light. There was a large laundry basket, a bucket and mop, and

some folding chairs. There was also a large me
plate on the wall.

The laundry chute.

"Go!"

The gun pressed into her ribs even harder and Caitlyn moved into the closet, Sam close at hand.

"Okay, through the chute. You first, lady."

Caitlyn froze.

"Did you hear me?" Hines demanded.

"Y-yes." She swallowed hard. Her legs wouldn't
move. She hated dark, closed spaces, nor could she
manage the water slides at the pool in the summer.
How could she plunge down a laundry chute like this?

"Get in, get in!" Hines shouted, waving the gun.

"Do it. Just go ahead," Sam whispered at her el-
bow. "I'm right behind you. We need to placate him
until I have time to think our way out of this."

"Okay." She took a deep breath. She trusted Sam.
And that trust was going to have to carry her through
this, otherwise Hines would shoot her in cold blood.

She was certain of it.

She went to the chute and put her hand on the cold
metal. She could do this. She had to do this. She'd
be fine. She'd seen them shove huge bags of towels
through the chute without a problem. Surely she'd fit
easily. And with any luck, the landing would be soft.

Maybe she and Sam could even get away.

She tucked her legs under her and sat at the top of
the slide. Then, closing her eyes, she pushed off, tum-
bling like Alice through the looking glass into the

kness. It seemed to go on forever, her head and ists and legs banging against the cold metal walls f the chute.

Finally she landed in a heap on a small pile of towels, not quite thick enough to cushion the blow. Without thinking, she scrambled out of the way just before Sam landed in the same spot.

"Let's run," she said to him. "Before Hines gets down here."

"Hines is already here," a voice said.

There was a thump behind them, and Branson Hines stood up, like a cartoon character who was able to fall off a cliff without getting hurt, and he smiled an ugly smile. "We're gettin' out of here," he said. He took handcuffs from his pocket and slapped the cold metal onto Caitlyn's wrist.

"What are you planning to do with us?" Sam asked angrily.

"Shut up!" Branson shouted, slapping the other side of the cuffs onto Sam's wrist.

Branson Hines led them to an ambulance and produced a set of keys. "Traveling in style, huh?" He grinned briefly. "Get in. Then you," he said to Caitlyn, "got a call to make."

"They just got a call from Caitlyn," Em said, holding out a cup of hot tea for Melanie. "Branson and Deena Hines are still demanding a baby in return for the hostages."

"Oh, no," Melanie groaned. "I hope they'll be all

right. The way he was waving that gun around…
She shuddered. "And that bomb. I don't even want
to think about what could have happened if someone
had tried to open the door to the storage room."

Jared smoothed her hair back. "Nothing would
have happened. The backpack was full of candy bars
and cans of soda Branson stole from the cafeteria."

"No bomb?" Melanie asked, her eyes wide.

Jared shook his head, then put his arm over her
shoulder and pulled her close. "If that was a bluff,
we can only hope that the rest of this is big talk, too.
Fortunately, the police have an idea of where they're
headed."

"Well, that's the best news I've had all day." Melanie put her head down on his shoulder, languishing
in the safety of his embrace. "This whole ordeal almost makes me want to get on that plane for England
tomorrow."

"Almost?" Jared repeated, turning her to face him.
"Does that mean you don't really want to go?"

She felt her face grow warm. "I've got the ticket
in my purse," she hedged. "Although my purse is in
the day-care center…"

"Do you want to go?" Jared's hands were firm on
her shoulders and he looked so deeply into her eyes
that she felt naked.

"Do you want me to?"

"No," he answered quickly. "God, no. I can't
think of any good reason for you to stay, though. I
know Mission Creek is a bit dull compared to what

ou're used to, and I'm not much of a draw, but I'll
o whatever it takes to make you happy if you'll just
give me a chance.''

Her mouth went dry. ''Jared, what are you saying?''

He took a deep breath. ''I'm saying I've been a
jerk and I know you probably want to get as far away
from me as possible, but I'm a jerk who's crazy in
love with you and if you'd even *consider* staying,
you'd make me the happiest man on earth.''

Happiness filled her like warm liquid. ''And what
if I do stay? What then?''

''Then I'll beg you to be my wife and move to that
house in the suburbs and start a family so we can
have barbecues on Sundays and eggnog on Christmas
mornings and a whole passel of kids to share it all
with.'' He cupped her face with his hands and kissed
her gently on the lips. ''Please say you'll stay.''

She wanted to say she would. She wanted to believe everything he said. But part of her was still
scared. ''Are you sure this is what you really want?''
she asked. ''Or does this have something to do with
the fact that something almost happened to me today
and it scared you?''

''This is *definitely* what I really want.'' He laughed.
''I love you, Melanie. I love you with all of my heart
and soul. You have a long and humiliating message
on your answering machine that should prove that
pretty nicely for you.'' He took her hands in his and
held them to his heart. ''I want you like I've never

wanted another woman in my life.'' He kissed her hands. ''Please say you'll marry me.''

''I will,'' she said, then gave a joyful laugh. ''I will. I love you, too, Jared, but there's something we need to talk about.''

''Kids, right?''

She froze. ''How did you know?''

''We've been talking about kids since we met,'' he said. ''Now, I know you decided that you didn't want to go through with the procedure, but that was when you were alone. If you're willing to change your mind about that and try again, I'm thinking we can start as soon as next month.''

Melanie's breath caught in her breast. ''So you don't know?''

He frowned and cocked his head. ''Don't know what?''

''Jared, I'm pregnant. That night we were to-gether...'' She shrugged. ''It was a one-in-a-million shot, but we did it.'' Her voice faltered.

''We did what?'' Jared asked carefully.

She pressed her lips together and willed her voice to work. ''We're going to have a baby.''

''Who is?''

''You and me.''

''You're *pregnant?*''

''Believe it or not, I am.''

His eyes went wide. ''Are you sure?''

She nodded and laughed.

He pulled her close and held her tightly. ''I can't

believe this. I just can't believe it. I mean, I looked at your chart. It's like a miracle.''

"There's no *like* about it," Melanie said. "It *is* a miracle.''

He drew back and looked into her eyes. "And you're absolutely one hundred percent positive.''

"Well, you're welcome to give me a thorough examination, Doctor. In fact, I hope you will. But yes, I'm sure. Ten pregnancy tests couldn't be wrong, could they?''

"You did *ten* tests?''

She shrugged and gave an embarrassed smile. "I couldn't believe the results the first nine times.''

"But the tenth—''

"Oh, yeah, the tenth I believed.''

He pulled her close and kissed her deeply. Her body responded like a match set to gasoline. She was in love. And she had the rest of her life to be kissed and held and loved by Jared. With children to love, too, her life would finally be complete.

"Come on," Jared said, taking her hand and helping her up. "Let's get out of here.''

"But Caitlyn and Sam—''

"I have a feeling Caitlyn and Sam will be fine in time," Jared said with confidence.

"You're sure?''

"Absolutely. At the moment, it's you I'm worried about. I want to take you home and put you to bed.''

She gave him a look.

"That's not what I mean," he said. "Although I'm

not averse to the idea. In the meantime, though, I want you to rest. We have a busy day tomorrow." He began to walk her down the hall.

"We do? What are we doing?"

"Looking for a house, buying some rings, getting married," he said, ticking the points off on his fingers. "A whole bunch of things."

"Getting married?" she repeated, giddy.

He stopped. "The courthouse is open from nine to five every day. Unless you'd prefer a big ceremony."

She shook her head. "Uh-uh. I've had enough pageantry in my life. I don't want a wedding, I want a marriage."

"You've got it," he said, kissing the top of her head. "And this one's going to last forever."

Epilogue

"Now if you don't like it, you have to tell me. I want you to be totally honest."

"All right." Melanie raised a hand to the blindfold over her eyes. "Can I take this thing off now?"

"Not yet," Jared answered, guiding her unsteady steps across some sort of pavement.

"Can you at least give me a clue as to where we are? That was a long car ride."

"It was ten minutes."

"Well, it seemed longer with a blindfold on."

He put his hands on her shoulders and moved her a couple of mini steps to the left. "Okay, that's perfect." He reached up and untied the blindfold, whipping it off with a flourish. "Here we are!"

It took her eyes a moment to adjust to the light of the bright, sunny day. But when they did, the sight before her made her gasp. It was a large white house, like something the Cleaver family might have chosen, with four windows across the second floor, and two large bay windows on the ground floor, flanking a double wooden entrance. The front yard was a wide sweep of green, shaded by large oak and cherry trees. A white fence bordered the property on a quiet tree-lined street. The driveway had been recently resurfaced, but the basketball net in front of the garage looked as if it had seen many games.

"What is this?" Melanie asked, hardly daring to hope.

"This," he said, "is just the front yard. Check out the back." He took her by the hand and led her around the side, past a tall magnolia tree and several fragrant rosebushes.

Next door, a man pushed a lawn mower and gave a friendly wave.

"That's Gary Mitchell," Jared said. "He and his wife, Liz, have lived here for eight years. They've got two kids, seven and four, and one on the way."

"Old friends of yours?" Melanie asked, raising an eyebrow.

"New," he said, leading her around the corner and stepping onto a slate patio with a large barbecue grill. "What do you think?" he asked, sweeping his hand to indicate a yard long enough to play pro football in.

"I think it's the most beautiful place I've ever seen," she answered, picturing children climbing in the old apple tree in the corner of the yard. "It's like something I've dreamed about."

"Good. Wait till you see the inside."

"Just a minute, Jared," she said, hanging back. "Tell me what's going on. What is this place?"

He gave her a quick kiss, then drew back, smiling more broadly than she'd ever seen. "It's my wedding gift to you, if you want it."

Her right hand flew automatically to the gleaming new gold band on her left ring finger. "A wedding gift? This house?"

"And the life that goes with it."

"Oh, Jared." She looked around at the place with new eyes. It really was a dream come true. This was the kind of place she'd longed for all her life, the kind of place where she could put down roots. A home with a heart, where she could spend the remainder of her days, cooking Thanksgiving dinners, filling Christmas stockings, hiding Easter eggs, lighting sparklers on the Fourth of July. She could see the scenes as clearly in her mind as if they were fond memories.

"Do you like it?"

"I love it."

"Think you can live here for forty or fifty years?"

She smiled and said, "Happily ever after."

* * * * *

*You will love the next story
from Silhouette's*
LONE STAR COUNTRY CLUB:

*THE LAWMAN
by Martha Shields
Available September 2002
(at Direct only)*

*Turn the page for an excerpt from this
exciting romance...!*

One

Tabitha Monroe knew the instant Assistant Chief of Police Jake White arrived. The tension filling the air changed so suddenly, so drastically, it was as if a hot South Texas wind had blown in from across the Rio Grande fifty miles to the west.

The police officials flanking her on the dais—from Mission Creek's well-staffed but hostage-inexperienced force—relaxed noticeably. They'd called Assistant Chief White in from his vacation and had been trying to put the press conference off until his return. But the media, which had been gathering from all over Texas throughout the day, had been clamoring for information.

The transformed air held more than relief, however. On top of the fear, concern and desperation inherent in a discussion of an armed madman disappearing with hostages floated an element of excitement, of restlessness that seemed almost…sexual.

Taken aback by the thought so inappropriate to the situation at hand—and so foreign to her personality— Tabitha hesitated in the middle of answering a question and scanned the crowd of reporters. They'd come from every news agency that could get a representative to Mission Creek in the three hours since news had leaked of the unusual hostage situation and kidnapping at Mission Creek Memorial Hospital. Her hospital.

Though she'd never met Jake White and had no idea what he looked like, she knew him the instant her gaze locked onto light-colored eyes framed with dark lashes.

Steady, strong, assessing, his gaze bored into hers and for an instant the rest of the room disappeared. A delicious shiver ruffled the hairs on Tabitha's skin, which became flushed with blood shot from a heart that suddenly beat as if her morning coffee had been laced with speed.

Now she knew where the sexual energy was coming from. It was as if he telegraphed desire across invisible wires stretching over the heads of the crowd.

From the corner of her eye, she saw Police Chief Burl Terry motion to his second-in-command to come forward.

"Miss Monroe?"

The reporter's voice barely penetrated Tabitha's frozen stupor.

What was wrong with her? Jake White was a *cop*. She'd never had a sexual thought about a cop in her life. She wasn't about to start now.

With an effort, Tabitha focused on the crowd of reporters and for an alarming instant couldn't remember the question she'd been answering or even the reporter who'd asked it. "Yes?"

Several people in the crowd were straining to see what she'd been staring at in the back of the room, but one young man in front helped her out by saying, "You were about to tell us what precautions the hospital was making to keep Branson Hines out."

"Thank you. Yes." Tabitha took a deep breath. "Mission Creek Police Chief Burl Terry has assured me that all entrances are sealed. Everyone will be searched when they enter Mission Creek Hospital, just as each of you were."

"Is that going to be enough?" asked another reporter, a woman from a national news agency. "Weren't Mission Creek police guarding the hospital against Mr. Hines when the bomb went off? He escaped several weeks ago, according to my sources."

Tabitha glanced at Jake White, who watched her intently, then at Chief Terry, who did not look pleased at having the quality of his men questioned.

Chief Terry stepped over to the microphone. "Your information is correct, as far as it goes. Hines was being escorted to the maximum-security prison in Lubbock by state troopers when he managed to escape."

Smiling with what she hoped looked like confidence, Tabitha returned to the mike when the chief stepped away. "I have every faith in the Mission Creek Police Department. It tells you something that Hines didn't attack until they'd cut back on security measures."

More hands raised immediately.

Tabitha pointed at another reporter, though all she wanted to do was end the press conference. She'd already said everything there was to say.

"The press conference is officially over."

The loud announcement from the back of the room startled everyone, including Tabitha. Since only one person could've given the command, her eyes immediately sought Jake White. He strode toward the podium, separating the crowd of reporters like Moses parting the Red Sea.

Every head in the room turned to watch him. Cameras tracked his progress to the dais. Reporters threw questions at him as he passed.

He ignored them all, just kept coming.

Chief Terry tapped Tabitha on the shoulder. Startled, she glanced at him. Since he obviously wanted the mike, she stepped back.

"Ladies and gentlemen," the chief said with obvious relief. "I'd like to introduce Assistant Police Chief Jake White of the Mission Creek Police Department. Assistant Chief White is a much decorated veteran of the Houston Police Department and has extensive experience in hostage situations. He's going to be the point man for the current crisis."

Assistant Chief White took the two steps leading up to the podium in one. Before turning to the crowd, he paused and met Tabitha's eyes.

Her breath froze in her lungs at the intensity in his pale-green eyes. The shouting of reporters dimmed to an indecipherable clamor—background noise that seemed to have nothing to do with them.

After what seemed like hours—but what in reality was probably just a few seconds—Jake gave her a small smile and nod, then turned away.

Air whooshed into Tabitha's lungs, sending shards of heat spiking through her. She knew the sudden flush would be evident on her pale complexion and was suddenly thankful that Jake was now in the spotlight instead of her. No matter how rudely he'd commandeered it.

For goodness' sake, what was wrong with her? She was in the most crucial situation she'd ever been in— would likely ever be in. A situation that could make or break her career as a hospital administrator. And she was acting about as professional as a teenager ogling a boy from behind the counter of a fast-food restaurant.

In walks Jake and—

Tabitha barely restrained a groan.

When had he become Jake instead of Officer White?

SILHOUETTE *Romance*

Escape to a place where a kiss is still a kiss...
Feel the breathless connection...
Fall in love as though it were
the very first time...
Experience the power of love!

Come to where favorite authors——such as
**Diana Palmer, Stella Bagwell,
Marie Ferrarella** and many more——
deliver heart-warming romance and genuine
emotion, time after time after time....

Silhouette Romance——
stories straight from the heart!

Silhouette®
Where love comes alive™

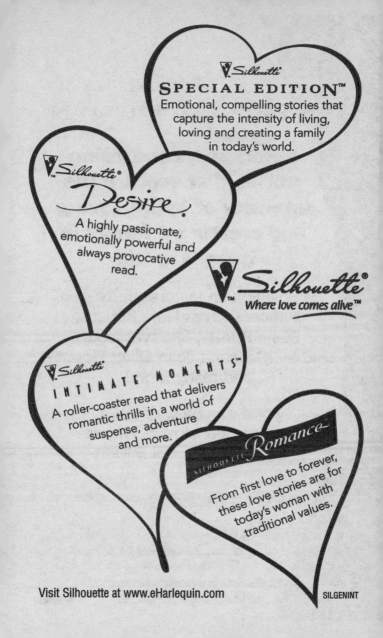

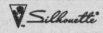